3/19

THE WORST IS YET TO COME

S.P. MISKOWSKI

TREPIDATIO
PUBLISHING

Trepidatio Publishing books may be ordered through booksellers or by contacting:
Trepidatio Publishing
www.trepidatio.com

JournalStone
www.journalstone.com

ISBN: 978-1-947654-46-4 (sc)
ISBN: 978-1-947654-47-1 (ebook)

Trepidatio rev. date: February 22, 2019

Library of Congress Control Number: 2018964301

Printed in the United States of America

Cover Art & Design: Mikio Murakami
Interior Layout: Jess Landry

Edited by Jess Landry
Proofread by Scarlett Algee

THE WORST IS YET TO COME

For my sister, Judy, with love.

THE CHILD was only two years old, too young to know where she was born. She didn't know her father's name, or her mother's. She didn't remember anything before that golden day in October, and of the day itself she only knew bits and pieces: the trip to Mc-Donald's; the playground surrounded by trees; jack o' lanterns lining a front porch; a dog barking and chasing a yellow ball; someone in a green raincoat leaning into the open car door to check the seatbelt, then gray-white ocean mist unraveling the coastline; a mountainous cloud casting a black shadow on the water; leaving the car in a parking lot at night; and finally, at the end, sleeping in a warm bed.

"This will be yours forever." She heard these words as she fell asleep.

Later, and for several years afterward, each time these scenes flickered across her memory she would touch the bracelet on her left wrist. It was a silver band with a sliding lock, engraved with the initial B. She would adjust the lock to make it fit, as she grew, and when her wrist was too large to wear the bracelet anymore, she wrapped it in a silk scarf and placed it in a drawer.

TASHA

THE MORNING they first noticed one another, they were changing clothes in the girls' locker room, the central portion of a dank warren of shower stalls and dressing areas one floor below the Clark Middle School gym. They tied blue laces on their Nikes and slouched morosely in identical P.E. uniforms—baggy, one-piece blue-gray jumpsuits that made them look like prison inmates. The locker room was alive with chatter about the spring dance, the newly created girls' basketball team, and the latest Netflix series featuring everyone's heartthrob, Noah somebody.

It was the time of year when purple crocuses began opening into the light. The shadows and angles of winter had softened, and there was a hint of tart Indian plum in the air. In the locker room, acrid sweat mingled with deodorant and jasmine body powder.

From opposite sides of the cramped room, they glanced across the swarm of girls and spotted one another, a sudden reflection—angular and awkward—without a mirror. Their pulses quickened in the same instant.

At least, that was how Tasha would remember it.

In one heartbeat she stood alone, dreading another boisterous gym class—dodging elbows while jogging, wincing at rope burns on her palms, gasping for breath after every fall from the balance beam onto the floor mat. In the next heartbeat she caught herself stupidly grinning across the locker room at this new girl, not caring what else might happen that day.

They had in common brown eyes and brown bobs, cut along the jawline and seldom brushed. Physically they could not have been more alien to the waxed and spray-tanned girls who surrounded them, fourteen-year-olds determined to achieve a new level of sophistication before high school.

To protect herself from the scrutiny and derision of her classmates, Tasha practiced a superior nonchalance, the attitude of one who had given up on the world so long ago it barely mattered anymore. It took all of her nerve to make eye contact. To her astonishment the new girl gave a silent shrug and grinned back at her. Half an hour later, while watching a classmate show off on the trampoline, they exchanged an eye roll.

The next day they acknowledged one another in homeroom. Over her shoulder, Tasha scanned the back row until she found her new friend, who signaled with a nod so slight anyone not paying close attention would have missed it. Tasha replied in kind.

On their third encounter, they spoke. It was a Friday afternoon, near the end of sixth period. Tasha was creeping through a vacant corridor with her backpack slung over one shoulder, sneaking out for the afternoon. She turned a corner and discovered Tyler Blanchard leaning against a row of lockers. A year older than Tasha, he was barrel-chested and broad-shouldered, but not very handsome.

On the floor beside him, Tasha's new friend crouched on her knees. With one hand Tyler was gripping her by the hair, forcing her down. His teeth and gums were bared in a hateful smile.

Tasha glanced at the empty corridor behind her, hoping despite her delinquency to see a teacher, the janitor, a hall monitor, anybody. There was no one. The three of them were alone.

Tasha froze. Tyler turned his grimacing smile toward her.

"What the fuck are you looking at, Natasha?" he asked. When the girl in his grip tried to stand, he shoved her down and mumbled, "Stay where you belong."

In the time it took him to say these words, Tasha rushed forward and slammed him in the chest with her backpack. He crashed against the lockers, but he was only startled for a second. Then he grabbed Tasha by the arm.

When he let go of her hair the new girl, still kneeling on the floor, bit his wrist with such ferocity that he let out a high-pitched, unmitigated shriek. The naked shock of it reverberated down the hall.

Tasha seized the chance to punch the side of Tyler's head. While he was wailing with one hand cupped over his ear, she caught her new friend by the jacket sleeve and the two girls ran, wild-eyed, elbows and knees pumping. They ran like crazy, not looking where they were going. They slammed open a set of double doors at the end of the hall and kept going.

They didn't slow down when they were out of the building and off school grounds. They ran down the road for half a mile, past the burnt-out shell of a diner where the name *Jessup's* could still be read in pale outline above the door. They darted over a hill to the backside of Curt Merritt's dilapidated barn. There, beneath the peeling strips of red and gray painted wood, they collapsed and sprawled on the cold ground to catch their breath.

They lay on their backs, staring up at the gray clouds wandering above. Nothing else moved for a minute or more. When they were able to sit up, face one another, and breathe normally, Tasha spoke first.

"That was *insane!*" she said. "What the hell was he trying to do?"

"No idea," said the new girl. "I don't even know him."

"Tyler's a jerk," said Tasha. "Everybody avoids him."

"I was leaving the bathroom. He came out of nowhere. Shit!" The new girl fished a green slip of paper from the pocket of her jeans. "I had a hall pass, too. Mr. Early's going to give me detention."

"Why? Tyler broke the rules. You should report him."

"I can't," said her new friend.

Tasha shook her head. "It's textbook MeToo. He was practically assaulting you on school property."

"I can take care of myself," said the girl, "but thanks." She stuck out her hand. "Briar."

Tasha knew her friend's name from homeroom but she didn't want to risk being a jerk by pointing it out. She had never known anyone called 'Briar,' but the sound of it was pleasing, somehow. She hesitated and then shook the girl's hand. "Tasha Davis. Nice to meet you."

"Oh, *formal* introductions. Okay," said Briar, which caused Tasha to blush. "I go by Kenny. Briar Kenny. But my real name is Gamel."

"Okay." Tasha nodded to show how cool she was with it, whatever it was.

"I'm not adopted," said Briar. "Kenny is my mom's boyfriend's name. It's a long story."

"No problem," said Tasha. She was afraid of asking too many questions. Her mom always did that, and she scared people away. More than anything, Tasha didn't want to scare Briar away. She fumbled for a reason to prolong the moment. "Hey, do you want to see something kind of weird but also pretty cool?"

Briar smiled. "Okay."

"Are you sure?" Tasha asked.

"Yeah," said Briar. "Why not?"

The two set off together. Tasha led the way through the damp grass of several deserted lots, circumventing the main road, where traffic was picking up as rush hour approached. They pushed aside branches and vines, and followed a dirt path into a patch of trees beginning to sprout new leaves.

This winding route took them to an abandoned residential street, where a handful of older homes had formed the basis for a neighborhood plan that never took off. It was one of many incomplete developments tucked in among the byways of Skillute. Some paths led nowhere and others went right up to a house, a back door with rusting hinges, or an iron gate consumed by ivy.

"I found this place accidentally, a couple of years ago," said Tasha.

"What is it?" Briar asked.

"Just a house, really," Tasha said. "Nobody's lived here for years, as far as I can tell." She stepped aside so Briar could get the full view.

The yard before them was filled with broken birdhouses and wooden windmills whose blue and yellow paint had faded from the weather. Every foot of space was taken up with whimsical garden furniture and bird feeders. In a far corner a pile of rusted gardening tools lay jumbled together, the edge of the shovel embedded in the dirt.

The cottage itself was sturdy, although the white paint and the blue and maroon trim had peeled. The property was surrounded by a low picket fence, splintered and cracked, the white paint spider-veined. With no occupied homes nearby, the place seemed all the more secret and lonesome.

Tasha took a step through the broken gate and beckoned for her friend to follow. Briar hesitated.

"It's okay," said Tasha, smiling. "The place is empty. I come here all the time. It's like my own private garden."

The girls wandered slowly through the weeds and ragged grass. Briar checked the front door and one of the boarded-up windows of the house. Both were solidly nailed shut.

"Who do you think lived here?" Briar asked.

"No idea," said Tasha. "I used to wonder about it. I imagined all kinds of things."

"A schoolteacher?"

"Maybe," said Tasha. "Or maybe a lonely guy, a lumberjack." She grinned.

"A lumberjack who carved birdhouses all winter."

"Sure," said Tasha. "If he got snowed in."

"I can see it, yeah," said Briar, smirking.

"Or maybe…"

"A witch," said Briar.

"Why do you say *that*?" Tasha asked.

"I don't know," said Briar. She turned around, making a sweeping motion with one hand at the piles of debris. "Think of all the migrating birds visiting this place in the winter. Think of how many years the birdhouses and feeders were here when the owner was alive. Now it's like a graveyard."

Tasha sat down on a wrought iron bench. The grass and weeds were so tall they grew between the slats in the middle, and she had to choose a bare spot. "I never thought about it that way, the history of it," she said. "I just think it's beautiful. I drew a sketch of the house last year for an art project. The teacher said it was kind of morose. She tried to talk me into adding sunlight, or a rainbow."

"Cheerful people are so weird," said Briar.

"I know, right?"

"Did you add a rainbow?" Briar smiled.

"Yeah," said Tasha. They laughed. "I didn't want her putting me on kid suicide watch, you know?"

"Ugh," said Briar, and they laughed again.

They examined a white wooden box surrounded by a tableau of brown and gray carved ducks, and another with a plump bluebird painted on the side. A rusty pinwheel creaked gently in the cool breeze. Some of the loose blocks of wood were impossible to identify, having fallen off of other structures or worked their way out from under various platforms built to support the birdhouses.

On either side of the rusty pinwheel stood a boy and a girl, their pallor and wasted limbs a stark contrast to the late afternoon sunlight streaking the garden, both of them invisible to Tasha and Briar. The boy and girl exchanged a glance, and the boy put a finger to his lips. This prompted a giggle from the girl, a sharp little outburst like the cry of a laughing thrush.

"Do you get the feeling something *bad* happened here?" Briar asked.

Tasha tilted her head and took a closer look around the yard. "Not really," she said. "It seems kind of peaceful to me."

Briar tore away a handful of the protruding weeds and grass, and sat on the bench. Both girls shivered at the passing of a cold current of air from the northwest.

"So," Tasha began. "You use the last name of—who is he again?"

"My mom's boyfriend," said Briar. She hunched her shoulders. "Rayburn Kenny." She waited as though she expected Tasha to recognize the name.

"Okay," said Tasha.

Briar's shoulders loosened a bit. "You've never heard of him?"

"Why?" Tasha asked. "Is he famous?"

"I guess not," said Briar. "I mean, I've never really believed him, but I kept hoping he wasn't a total creep—you know, lying to my mom about things that didn't even matter."

"Did he say he was famous?"

"He says a lot of stuff," said Briar. "Most of the time he hints around, name-dropping and making it seem like he knows all of these people he probably only met once."

"Did you Google him?"

Briar shrugged. "I don't exactly have a computer of my own."

"Not exactly?" Tasha wrinkled her nose. "I thought everybody had two or three."

"My mom lets me use her laptop when she's at home. When she feels like it."

Tasha held up her phone and raised her eyebrows.

"No," said Briar. "We only have a landline."

Tasha's jaw dropped in mock surprise. "Jesus! Who *are* you, Briar Gamel Kenny?"

"I know," said Briar with a sheepish grin. "I know." She shook her head. "I should live in a museum."

"It isn't that bad," said Tasha. "I mean, yeah, the only time I've ever been without a phone, I was grounded. But that's about my mom, more than me. She likes me to 'check in.' As a matter of fact..." She unlocked the screen, typed a quick text message, and sent it. She nodded after the signal. "There we go. Now I don't have to hurry home. Do you need to text your mom?" She smiled at the phone and held it out to Briar, then remembered. "Oh, right," she said. "I guess she doesn't have a cell phone either."

"It's no big deal," said Briar. "Don't tell my mom, but I started using the computers at the school library. She doesn't even know they exist! They're pretty restricted, but if you're not a gamer and you're not after porn, they're good enough. I did a search yesterday and I found Ray's name listed on a couple of albums."

"So he isn't a total liar?" Tasha asked.

"No," said Briar. "But I don't think anybody's ever heard of him. He's just a back-up musician, a guy who gets hired to play guitar with a bunch of people in a studio. Or he used to get hired. He told my mom he toured with Blake Shelton and some other country singer."

"I don't know who Blake Shelton is," said Tasha.

"And *you* have a phone and a laptop," said Briar, smirking.

"Sorry," said Tasha. "I know. I'm so typical, it's embarrassing."

Briar shook her head. From across the yard the pallid boy and girl studied the two teenage girls seated together on the bench, as if they were examining a work of art for the first time.

"Are you sure," Briar said to Tasha, "you don't feel something—*creepy*—here? Something *not right*?"

"No," said Tasha. "I come here whenever I want to be alone. It's a little strange, I guess, but it's quiet."

"Skillute's pretty quiet all over," said Briar.

"How long have you lived here?" Tasha asked.

"Only a few weeks. What about you?"

"We moved from Seattle years ago," said Tasha. "When I was little."

"Oh, wow, why would anybody leave Seattle for this place?" Briar asked.

"You know," said Tasha. "Fresh air, less crime, no drugs..."

"The usual suspects," said Briar. She fished a joint and a lighter from the pockets of her jeans. She offered both with a little flourish, but Tasha declined.

"Where did you live before this?" Tasha asked while Briar touched the end of the joint to the sputtering flame.

"Everywhere," said Briar, and exhaled. The smoke drifted around her shoulders and faded away. "Ray says we're like that Johnny Cash song, because we've been everywhere. Like I said, he's a liar. But we've lived in four towns since he met my mom. That includes Tacoma, where my mom and I lived alone until a couple of years ago. She says we're gypsies, but really, we just go wherever she can find a job."

"What does she do?"

"Dog grooming," said Briar. "I know, it's pretty gross."

"No," said Tasha. "I don't think so."

"You don't live with it. Her hair smells like dog fur when she comes home," said Briar. "She has to shampoo with this special kind of gel, it's so sweet, it's like pouring honey right on your hair. Anyway, she works at Rose Valley Mall." She shook her head and then studied the ground. "What do your parents do?"

"My dad sells construction equipment to contractors, sometimes from an office and sometimes from home. I'm not even sure what kind. He never talks about it. He travels, but only for a day or two at a time. My mom does graphic design. She used to paint…"

Briar held out the joint. "Used to?"

"She claims her work was never any good," said Tasha, accepting the joint without lighting it.

"Why?"

"She couldn't sell anything. Well, one time she sold a painting to a rich woman from Vancouver. The woman bought it off the wall at a café or some place. I think this was before I was even born. Nothing since. She designs logos and websites for people. She never meets her clients in person. They Skype. It's kind of boring, but she likes it."

"Well," Briar said, "at least she's an artist of some kind, right? What my mom does is *really* boring. And the car smells like wet dogs all the time, and we don't even have a dog."

"What's your stepdad's name again?"

"Ray," said Briar. "Rayburn Kenny. He's not my stepdad, just a guy my mom picked up at a bar. Now he lives with us. He said he had his own band, but his band mates cheated him, so he quit. I bet that's a lie, too."

"What does your mom do when he lies about stuff?"

"Nothing. See, Ray's always got another story. Last fall my mom said she was fed up with all the traveling and she wanted her own home again. All of a sudden Ray said he had a good friend in real estate, and the guy could get him a good deal on a place in this little town called Skillute. Made it sound like a Disney movie, right, with bluebirds and daisies? 'A perfect place for kids and families.' So my mom packed up and we moved—for the third time. Now we're staying in this dump, in a *trailer park*. Ray keeps saying it's only temporary while our 'real house' is being renovated, but I don't believe it. We've never even seen it! Every time my mom brings it up, he has another excuse."

"Wow," said Tasha. "So why are you supposed to use his name, again?"

Briar looked away. Tasha touched her hand and passed the joint back.

"Sorry," said Briar. "It's a long story."

"No problem," Tasha said.

"And really," said Briar, "thanks. I mean it."

"Huh?"

"The Tyler thing," said Briar.

"No worries. If not me, you know, somebody else would have come along."

"Maybe. Maybe not," said Briar. "If *nobody* came and that creep wouldn't let go, I might've had to kill him or something, to get away." She studied Tasha's expression, and added, "and then I'd go to prison and I'd have to wear a P.E. uniform forever." She laughed.

Tasha squinted and pulled her sweater tight around her shoulders. "I don't know," she said, playing along. "Murder's kind of extreme. Don't you think you could just castrate him?"

"Sure," said Briar. "At the very least, I could kick him in the balls."

"Classic self-defense," Tasha said with a grin. "Like everything we did to him back there. 'It was self-defense, your honor.'"

"Do you think he'll tell someone?" Briar asked with her head cocked to one side. Tasha couldn't tell if she was serious or still kidding.

"No," said Tasha. "Tyler's not going to admit two girls beat him in a fight."

"We did," said Briar with a broad smile. "We beat him!"

"Yeah, we did," said Tasha, beaming.

Briar laughed and shook her head. "Oh my god, did you hear him scream?"

"Like a baby!" Tasha laughed.

"Like a little bitch!"

"Oh. My. God," said Tasha, her eyes wide. "We made Tyler Blanchard scream like a bitch!"

"What is he, anyway? A football player or something?" Briar asked. "He seems like he's had a few brain injuries."

"No, he's just naturally stupid. He was held back in, like, fourth grade for never doing his homework and stealing money from the school janitor. He's still the 'most tardy and/or absent' kid in the whole school. He's spoiled. His mom has money and she travels all the time. When he bothers to show up, he just wanders around acting like a Trump. The hall monitors hate him. They actually hide from him."

Both girls shivered. The temperature was dropping, although the sunlight hadn't yet faded. A fragrance of wet cedar wafted in from a patch of woods.

Briar stood and brushed bits of dirt and leaves from her jeans. "Sorry. I have to get home."

"Okay," said Tasha. She stood, and they turned toward the garden gate. "Hey, what would you have done, really, if you had to fight Tyler by yourself?"

"I have a couple of talents," said Briar.

"Yeah?" Tasha gave her friend a sly smile. "For example?"

"Look. If you stab *here* with a sharp enough knife," said Briar, pointing to a spot on Tasha's inner thigh, "the creep dies in a few minutes. Even without any poison on the blade. And it doesn't have to be a big knife, just really sharp. It's all in the wrist, and how deep you can jab him. Trust me. He'll bleed out. I read about it in one of Ray's survival manuals."

"If you had a knife, yeah," Tasha said.

Briar reached inside her jacket and pulled out a Swiss Army knife. The red handle was chipped in a couple of spots. She took only a second to isolate the blade she wanted, and she held it up proudly.

"You carry this around at school?" Tasha asked.

"You never know when you might have to kill somebody," said Briar with a wink.

Tasha looked into her new friend's eyes and then noticed the smile sneaking in. Both girls smiled.

The pallid boy and girl stood flanking the gate. They gave one another a solemn nod, a silent confirmation as Briar and Tasha exited.

BRIAR

THEY WERE brother and sister, only eighteen months apart in age, and dead for the past six years. Their hair matched the color of wet straw. Their chins were smudged with dirt the same shade and chemical composition as that in the garden.

The boy, Orton, was a little taller than his sister. He wore cargo pants and a moth-eaten *Spider-Man* T-shirt.

The girl, Gretchen, wore a cotton dress with a faded, watery print. She kept smoothing the fabric and checking the buttons. She clutched a bouquet of shriveled blackberries, dead vines, and nightshade in one hand. Dried blood mottled her skin from the wrist to the fingertips.

Orton and Gretchen studied the two teenage girls, who were picking bits of grass and leaves from their clothes. They watched the girls exit through the garden gate, saw them say goodbye at the main road and head in opposite directions.

Gretchen waited for her brother to choose. When Orton followed the girl in the jacket and jeans, Gretchen went along, trailing a few feet behind and slapping at the ground with her dead bouquet.

They traveled this way—Briar in front, unaware of her invisible entourage, ignoring passing cars on the main road and stopping to study every vacant lot, while the two pale-skinned urchins tagged along after her. They walked for a mile until they reached a metal and cedar arch displaying the name of a mobile home park.

Briar continued beneath the sign and into the park. Orton and Gretchen stared after her for a long time. Finally Gretchen sighed.

"Want to go follow that other one?" she asked. "The one with the backpack?"

"Nah," said Orton. "This is the one. She's no good, you'll see."

"But we can't even get in there," said Gretchen, pointing at the trailer park.

"Betcha there's a witch livin' in there somewhere," Orton told her. "That's why."

Gretchen frowned. "So what are we supposed to do?"

"Wait," said her brother. He picked up a piece of gravel and pitched it into the trailer park. "Lots of things can happen. Let's see what the bad one gets up to."

Gretchen sighed heavily. "I hate waiting," she said. She turned on her heel and wandered off to gather more dead weeds.

* * *

The gravel slipped this way and that beneath Briar's shoes. It was a greeting she dreaded each time she entered the park and headed down the path to the Kenny lot: the crunch of gravel. This was the first sound she'd noticed the day they moved in, forever tied to her misery and her mother's pitiful attempts at concealing disappointment.

Everything about the Maplewood Mobile Home Park was unbearable. Not shabby or rundown, but horribly cute, smug, and boring. Most of the lots were cluttered with the garden gnomes, ceramic toadstools, and white picket fences of elderly people Briar hated, especially the woman next door who went by the name Mrs.

Ted Van Devere. Silver aluminum wind chimes hung from every corner of her yard, and they shivered at the slightest breeze. The air outside her mobile home reeked of lavender. This was a scent Briar associated with age and death, though she didn't know why. She thought of the neighbor as Mrs. Dead Lavender.

Briar pushed the gravel around with the toe of one shoe and stared at the door to the Kenny home. She could already hear Ray practicing guitar, and she knew he'd be waiting in the living room, taking up as much space as possible.

She could only dream of having her own private bedroom again, like the one in Tacoma. With each move the possibility had become more remote, until she ended up sleeping on a fold-out sofa. She lowered her expectations and started hoping for a separate bathroom someday, where she wouldn't have to clean up Ray's mess before she could brush her teeth.

The trailer park was the fourth place they'd lived since the night Evelyn Gamel had seen Rayburn Kenny playing guitar for a drunken folk singer in a tavern. Ray had moved in with them a week later, dragging along three broken guitars, two duffel bags full of dirty clothes, a library of tattered paperbacks, and a never-ending sense of disruption and uncertainty.

Before Ray invaded their lives, they had been alone together, Briar and her mother Evelyn, for as long as the girl could remember. "This is where we're going to be forever, the two of us," Evelyn used to say when she tucked Briar in for the night. "Just you and me."

Evelyn had spent her days shampooing, trimming, and babysitting dogs at Mutt Heaven to pay the rent on a tiny bungalow on a tree-lined street in Tacoma. They were happy, the two of them. Evelyn said this almost every day—"We're happy like this, right?"

Briar would nod and say yes, yes, they were happy. She didn't know what else to say. She couldn't remember a time or a place before the bungalow in Tacoma with its trim lawn and maple trees, bright kitchen with red tiles, and her little bedroom—although a sudden change of light or a burst of fragrance might conjure feelings she couldn't attach to anything.

As soon as she was old enough, Briar cleaned house and cooked meals—lunch or dinner or both, depending on Evelyn's schedule and mood. She pulled weeds in the front yard and raked up leaves in the fall. She learned to help change the oil in Evelyn's ratty old Chevy. She kept up with her homeschool lessons by studying at night, since Evelyn would only let her use the secondhand laptop when she was at home.

In every way Briar tried to help out, to not be a burden or a nuisance. Something tickled the edges of her awareness, and she knew she could be left behind or forgotten, cut adrift, if she didn't prove her value. There was no doubt in her mind Evelyn loved her, but she also loved stupid things like chocolate chip ice cream. She'd thrown a raving fit in the kitchen one night after dinner, when she discovered they only had chocolate ripple in the freezer. When Briar offered to walk to the grocery store and buy the right kind, Evelyn grew more agitated and angry. That's how she could be—cozy and playful, then cold and manic, shrieking about angels and ice cream and ungrateful daughters.

Then came the night—Briar was twelve-and-a-half—when their lives changed and never got better again. Not that everything had been ideal before, but she'd been able to rely on Evelyn to keep a regular schedule and a roof over their heads. Once Evelyn fell in love, nothing was guaranteed anymore.

Reluctantly, Evelyn had joined a co-worker for a drink at the Dockside Tavern. It was the first time she had gone out at night in years. Something about Ray Kenny's scroungy beard and shoulder-length ponytail, and the way he stared at her while playing, made a part of Evelyn's brain fizzle and snap like a broken toaster. Briar imagined sparks coming out of her mother's ears and nose whenever she spoke to Ray on the phone.

They called one another 'Evvy' and 'Ray-Ray.' They drank beer all week. Sometimes Evelyn missed work, and it cost them dearly, since she was the only one with a steady job and she was paid by the hour. They lived on TV dinners and fast food. They shopped at flea markets and spent all of Evelyn's savings on damaged guitars. Ray's master plan was to refurbish what he called 'discarded classics' and resell them for profit. To date they had bought seventeen guitars, and he'd never so much as changed the strings on most of them.

Now, in the trailer, the guitars stood propped against the walls and clustered in corners and closets. The guitars were the reason Briar couldn't have even a little space, a private area of her own. Lately Ray had begun talking about building a shed out back, to 'expand the collection,' but he never got around to doing any of the things he promised.

Ray and Evelyn had claimed the only bedroom. 'Ray-Ray' snored so loudly all night Briar could hear him from her sofa bed in the living room. He ate cereal in his underwear. He swiped money from Evelyn, so Briar swiped weed from him. She never cleaned house or cooked a meal anymore, not for the benefit of 'Ray-Ray.' Not for the man who had stolen her mother and her life.

Gone were the pop tunes mother and daughter used to hum in the car, half serious and half joking. The radio was set to a modern country station. Every time Briar changed it, someone changed it right back.

Worst of all was the way her mother dressed. There was an edge of desperation to it that made Briar feel queasy. It was the reason Briar demanded a tattoo, something dark and dumb and guaranteed to freak her mother out. She carefully selected a pattern of dead leaves and shriveled vines from the cover of an album Ray hated. To her shame and amazement, Evelyn was fine with the idea and even went along to lie about Briar's age. She could still feel the shock of the needle burning into her skin. Girls her age were not supposed to have dead things painted on them.

"You're embarrassing," she told Evelyn once. They were standing in the parking lot at Safeway with a cart full of ground beef, hot dogs, chips, and the brand of beer Ray liked. Evelyn was dressed in a red satin cocktail dress she'd bought for ten bucks at the Salvation Army. It was at least half a size too tight. Her hair was tucked up into a messy French bun, and she balanced unsteadily on black high heels.

"You look like trash," Briar said, and Evelyn slapped her.

Nearby, a bearded man in knit pants and a cardigan began dialing a number on his phone. Evelyn caught sight of him and grabbed Briar by the elbow.

"Get in the car," she hissed.

Evelyn tore out of the lot and merged with traffic, doing about ten miles above the limit. They were halfway home before they noticed they'd forgotten the groceries.

It wasn't the only time they'd dropped what they were doing to make a run for it, although it happened less and less often. When Briar was little, they'd done it frequently enough that she recognized the signals. The cause might be Evelyn herself, tossing a tube of lipstick or mascara into her purse and dodging a cashier. Or they might have to slip out of a restaurant by the back door after a hearty meal Evelyn couldn't afford.

There were also the sudden departures Evelyn attributed to the 'heebie jeebies,' when something unseen caused a shiver to run through her and Briar could tell, by the frantic look in her eyes, they had to find the nearest exit. After one of these dashes Evelyn would be paranoid for days, peeking out of the curtains, ducking her head and hiding behind sunglasses on her way to the car.

Briar never understood her mother's fear, but she never questioned it. If she tried to recall every detail about where they were and what was happening, she might remember a glance from a stranger at another table, or a whispered conversation between women studying the screen of a smart phone. But the incident in the Safeway parking lot was the first in a long time.

* * *

"Hey there, Miss Britney," said Ray as soon as Briar walked through the door of their trailer home. "What did you learn at school today, Brit?"

It was a joke he hauled out at least once a week. Since the day they met, he'd been telling Briar she should change her name to Britney. "If you ever want to have a stage career, it's a lot more commercial. What kind of name is Briar? It sounds like Snow White or that other cartoon bitch, the one with the big horns."

Names were a sore point. As soon as Ray moved in, Evelyn had dropped 'Gamel' and adopted his surname. She insisted Briar do the same thing. "If you want to be like other kids your age and fit in, you need to be presentable."

Briar didn't know what Evelyn meant by this. When they moved from Tacoma to Spanaway to Tumwater, Briar continued home-schooling. Once they settled in Skillute, with Kenny as their family name and Ray as a fake father, she was enrolled mid-year at Clark Middle School. There she floated through her days in a fog, never certain how to behave or what to say to her eighth grade classmates. She was assigned an advisor, but the woman was goofy and made her feel irritable instead of confident. Tasha Davis was the first girl who'd ever regarded Briar with something other than anger or pity.

Briar's fourteenth birthday had come and gone without comment last summer, or maybe her fifteenth would occur in the spring. Evelyn had always been fuzzy about the date, and Briar was afraid to ask why. She didn't ask about the proof, the documents that must have been submitted to get her into Clark. She had *never* asked. To question her mother's methods was to court madness, screaming fits, sleepless nights, and sullen days. It was always better not to go down that road.

"Hey, Brit," said Ray. "You should smile more."

"Hey, Mr. Burns," Briar replied. "You should get a place to live."

Ray chuckled and shook his head. "I still don't get your sense o' humor, girl," he said. "Come on, let's see a little bitty smile..."

As usual, he was wearing a T-shirt and boxer shorts, sitting on the foldout sofa Briar used as a bed. His legs were spread wide. On one knee he balanced his acoustic guitar, the only one with new strings. He plucked and slapped out a rhythm, something bluesy and almost decent, before he segued into the opening chords of a syrupy country song.

"Oh, Lord," he sang. "Oh, Lord!"

"Oh, Lordy Lord!" Briar mock-wailed as she stomped down the hall and locked herself in the bathroom.

She sat on the floor and closed her eyes. She would stay like this for an hour, until her mother arrived home from work.

Lately Ray had begun to touch her whenever he felt like it, if her mother wasn't home. So far it had stopped at a hand on the shoulder, a pinch to the thigh, or a poke in the ribs, but it made her jump. She didn't know which way to turn to avoid him. He seemed to be everywhere. She'd begun to slouch, with her arms crossed over her chest, when she was at home. Almost as bad as the grabbing and teasing was the fear gnawing away at her stomach, the fear that Evelyn would choose Ray if Briar told her. She was afraid and ashamed of being afraid.

"Let him die," she whispered to herself. "Let him set himself on fire and die."

She heard the dull thud-thud-thud of his fist on the bathroom door.

"Hey, little girl," he said. "You're gonna have to open up. I've gotta pee real bad."

Briar bit her lower lip.

"Real bad! Oh Lord, I'm about to die!"

Briar said nothing.

"You want me to go outside?" he asked. "On the doorstep? In front of the neighbors?"

"Go away," she told him. "Fucking pig," she said under her breath.

She heard him chuckling. Then he was moving, walking away.

"You're no fun," he called over his shoulder. "No fun at all, Britney!"

The wobbly chords of another country song told her he was returning to his guitar in the living room. He would be playing when Evelyn came home. He always got the most attention possible with the least effort.

Briar sighed with relief. She was out of the spotlight for a while.

KIM

THE DAVISES were the kind of people their friends described as a perfect family. But most of their friends lived back in Seattle, one hundred and sixty miles north of the rural-suburban town where Kim and Charles had carved out a home.

The Davis family had relocated when Tasha was old enough for elementary school. Back then, Skillute seemed remote, a pastoral oasis. These days it was more in flux. People still waved a quaint hello at traffic intersections and greeted neighbors while shopping. But everyone also seemed to be recycling, eating artisan bread, and signing up for Zumba classes at Rose Valley Mall.

If Kim and Charles had paid closer attention, they might have noted the abundance of miniature U.S. flags in shop windows, on car bumpers, and on porches year-round. They might have realized that when locals referred to 'those people up north,' they weren't speaking of Alaskans or Canadians. 'Up north' was Seattle, a place middle-aged people were leaving in droves.

Some moved south to retire. Others fled because of the housing market. In 2009, Kim Davis told all of their friends in Seattle she'd read a magazine article comparing school systems and decided on the spot to relocate for the sake of their beautiful daughter, Tasha.

Kim inherited a small trust fund from her grandmother; nothing exceptional, but enough to make the down payment on the house in Skillute with its cedar and glass walls, wraparound deck, and a half-acre of land. From the beginning, the Davises were out of step. None of their new neighbors came right out and said it was strange for a local to hire a gardening service, but the suppressed smile or an amused tilt of the head were enough to let Kim and Charles know they were a bit extravagant by Skillute standards.

Aside from a few people they met at the gym, the Davises made no friends in their adopted town. Over the years, they established the habit of spending their weekends and nights at home. Charles kept his business trips to a minimum.

Tasha had music and dance lessons, but never took an interest in sports. Kim was silently grateful. She made a point of attending Tasha's lessons, and she shared her daughter's disdain for teams and for traveling to away games.

The family enjoyed the occasional day trip together, but mostly they barbecued and watched movies at home. It was a life more insular than Charles ever imagined, but since he was the one who'd been most gung-ho about raising a family, he kept any restless urges to himself. As for politics, he tried not to think about how his neighbors voted in the last election.

He would never forget that evening two years ago, on November 7th, when he had stopped by Trader Joe's to pick up Gruyère and eggs for crepes. As he passed the nice lady who prepared the daily food samples, he asked her casually if she was excited to cast her vote the next morning. The nice lady popped the top on a tin of ready-made guacamole and said yeah, she sure as heck was.

"Great," said Charles. "It's been a rough year, hasn't it? I think Clinton can use all the help she can get right now." He was only making conversation. The swift reply left him confused. When he told the story to Kim later that night, she said she felt a little sick to her stomach.

"If that whore wins the election, I don't know what I might do," said the nice lady.

Since that moment, there had been nights when Charles could barely sleep. Lately he found there were evenings when he could only relax after two or three glasses of Burgundy. When the cashiers at the store started giving him a hard look while ringing up his weekly purchases, he joined a wine club that delivered. He knew he was creating a greater distance between himself and his neighbors, but he couldn't stop himself.

Kim, too, had drifted further from social life after the election. Making the down payment on their house had depleted her trust fund. Her contribution to the household budget came from clients online. Lately she'd begun to rely exclusively on Facebook and Twitter for social connection. By subscribing to streaming services, she eliminated the need to visit the only DVD rental store in town. Then she discovered she could order paper towels, toilet paper, and tampons to be delivered. She only had to face people outside her family when she shopped for groceries, and then she avoided conversation.

Back when Tasha was in first grade, Kim had made one brief attempt at connecting with other parents. She had attended parent-teacher night and a couple of fundraisers. At one of these events, she was taken under the commanding wing of another mom, a stocky, immaculately-groomed woman named Wendy with twin sons, Anders and Benjamin, and a husband who was a wildly successful day trader.

Wendy was described as a 'go-getter' by the other parents. She took an interest in every aspect of her sons' lives, from soccer to choir practice. She volunteered for bake sales and talent shows. Everyone admired and feared Wendy, and everyone loved her wry sense of humor. What they didn't mention, and some didn't seem to notice, was that Wendy was a remorseless bigot.

"I can see my boys will have to step up their math game," she whispered to Kim at a meet and greet. "They're barely up to speed on subtraction." She nodded in the direction of the only Korean-American girl in the class. When Kim realized what Wendy meant, she felt like she'd been punched in the gut.

"I don't think they need to worry much about math until third grade," was all she could think of to say.

The friendship lasted four excruciating months. Over coffee, at lunch, or chatting on the phone, Wendy made Kim a mortified witness to all of her views on parenting and life.

Before the twins came along, Wendy claimed, she and her husband had never thought of leaving Portland, where they had friends, a network of contacts, and a sweet, rambling apartment in an ivy-draped brick building. It was the life they'd dreamed of, both idyllic and modern.

Then came the day when little Anders' backpack was stolen at pre-school, later found torn to shreds on the playground. He refused to name the kid who took it from him. Two nights later over dinner he asked what 'juvie' was, prompting a series of 'discussions, not arguments' between his nervous parents.

"It's only a word," Wendy's husband had said. "Maybe we're overreacting."

"These are our children," Wendy had to remind him. "Nothing we do for their sake is an overreaction."

In bed with the lights out, they couldn't stop talking about it, Wendy said. All of their previously unspoken fears seemed to be coming true.

At this point in Wendy's tale, Kim interrupted for clarification. Exactly what was it Wendy and her husband feared?

"The boys were in pre-school," Wendy said. "This was the time when their minds should have been open to nature and music and art, not penalties for misdemeanors."

"I'll bet one of the kids in their group heard it from an older sibling," said Kim. This seemed reasonable enough.

"Right," Wendy said. "But it pulled their attention in the wrong direction, you see? And it was only going to get worse. One of the other moms told me her boys were propositioned by a drug dealer, another student at their school."

"And that's why you decided to move?" Kim asked.

"We had to consider all the people our children were going to come into contact with, living in a city. The population density and all of the influences, you just know drugs are going to be an issue. And if drugs are in the picture, you're going to get a different level of violence. And none of it was going away anytime soon. Not with a, you know, *Democrat* in the White House."

"Are we talking about...?" Kim said and then hesitated. "This isn't about, you know, *race*, is it?" She remembered flinching at the word even as she said it.

Wendy's answer was immediate. "No, no," she said. "Of course not. Why would you say that?"

"The whole thing is about...?"

"Standards," Wendy said. "A way of looking at the world. It's about our children and their future. It's about what we want our children to learn."

"Values?" Kim asked, and felt her mouth going dry. How many times had she and Charles laughed at the term, and criticized the way it served as a shield to starchy politicians and feel-good TV celebrities when they wanted to trash other people or make racist assumptions?

"Right," said Wendy without a trace of irony. "That's right. It's about our core values."

* * *

"Are they just blind to their own privilege? Are they crazy? Did they run away from the city looking for some white fantasy utopia with rolling lawns and singing bluebirds?"

These were questions Kim asked Charles after she decided to avoid Wendy and her family. Charles poured another glass of wine and said, "All of us are running away from something, right?"

None of the questions they asked made them feel better about where they lived and what they were doing with their lives. They had come to Skillute for peace and quiet. They had come here to be better people. They had tried to think of the town as a healing place where they could start over. There were times, recently, when Kim could think of nothing else, when she sat alone staring out the living room window past the deck to her impeccable garden while Charles was at the office and her daughter, the child for whom they had sacrificed everything, was at school.

The Davises were, after all, safe. Was there something fundamentally bad about seeking safety for the sake of one's family? Wasn't that why they'd moved eight years ago, to a comfortable and characterless town anchored on three sides by gargantuan shopping malls?

The past two years had been challenging, and sometimes frightening. In some ways, it was both more enlightening and more disturbing than anything the Davises had experienced before.

Kim had long ago stopped hanging around with Wendy. And yet, she was afraid to delete the woman from her Facebook friend list. The thought had crossed her mind a hundred times. She hadn't been able to do it, and she wasn't sure why. It was embarrassing to think she might be afraid of the woman, afraid an outright rejection might prompt Wendy to gossip online about the Davis family and their politics and their only child.

Meanwhile Wendy, who'd become dismayed by 'the diversity issue' the year she spotted two children of color in the twins' class, had moved her family to a remote, luxurious cabin where she took up knitting and homeschooled her boys until they were old enough to attend Clark. At that point, she judged they were sufficiently well trained to pick their way through a dangerous world by shoving aside other people's ideas, and she sent them back to mingle with their classmates.

"To complete their socialization," Wendy posted online. "After all, I won't be here to protect them forever. They need to know how to network in real life."

In their youth the Davises had believed most people wanted the same things, that they might disagree on certain issues, but everyone was moving in the same general direction, making slow but gradual progress toward a hazy future somehow magically balanced between equality and prosperity. Following the 2016 election, TV pundits based in cities thousands of miles away assured the Davises that the current crisis, the rift revealed by the election, was their fault and the fault of people like them. They were over-educated and over-paid. They wanted too much. They were greedy, arrogant, and lazy. They didn't understand working people, the salt of the earth individuals who made up the backbone of the nation. People like the nice lady who demonstrated how to prepare tacos at Trader Joe's.

The Davises were too sophisticated for their own good, the finger-wagging pundits said. They'd grown complacent and had come to believe, in a drowsy and disconnected state of mind, that everything everywhere was getting better without their help or involvement. They were the kind of people who donated to ACLU and Planned Parenthood and allowed themselves to drift into greater and greater comfort while pretending not to care about money. Why worry, such people believed, back when the country was finally grown up enough to elect a black man president? Surely it wasn't necessary to become activists just to get clean water, safe bridges and roads, and decent schools.

After the presidential election, the Davises soon grew weary of conversation with their old friends back in Seattle. They tweeted cheerful memes instead, and silently cringed when even their liberal acquaintances offered 'hopes and prayers' in response to every bit of bad luck, every horrific news article.

Fearful assumptions that had long ago settled into the ash and soil of places like Skillute had been stirred up and raked to the surface. Along with natural apprehension and a newly awakened wariness of the unknown, the Davises began to question themselves, their ideals, their hopes for the future. All they knew for certain was that they couldn't go back the way they had come. The city where they'd spent their youth was a different world now. They couldn't afford to live there anymore, even if they wanted to.

BRIAR & TASHA

ON SATURDAY afternoon the girls visited the birdhouse garden again. Then they walked aimlessly through the sparse woods and vacant developments, taking every detour, every winding path. The ditches on both sides of the roads were filled with bright puddles of rainwater. The spring air was cold with the promise of more rain.

On the major roads, the cars passed with a smooth swish of tires over wet asphalt. Nobody traveled the side roads if they didn't live nearby, aside from delivery trucks and people who'd taken the wrong freeway exit. It was something the Davises had talked about endlessly before moving here. Charles had convinced Kim it was safe. In this town their daughter would have the freedom to wander a little, outdoors, without constant supervision. Charles was insistent. A bit of independence was crucial to Tasha's development. After all that had happened in their lives, how could they deny her this?

Tasha's raincoat was buttoned up to her chin. Briar let her jacket hang loose, exposing a tattoo of ivy and dead leaves on the side of her neck. Tagging along behind them, Orton and Gretchen wore what they'd worn the day before, what they always wore: the grass-stained *Spider-Man* T-shirt and baggy cargo pants on the boy, the faded print dress on the girl. Gretchen carried her dead bouquet before her, playing bridesmaid until Orton gave her a stern look.

"What did you think this time?" Tasha asked. "Is the place growing on you?"

"Well," said Briar, "I can see how the house used to be sort of pretty. But I still think the garden's kind of weird."

"You like it, though?"

"Sure," said Briar. "Anyway, everything is weird, if you think about it."

Tasha laughed. "Everything?"

Briar pointed to a tree with entwined limbs. "What's that?" she asked.

"Some kind of oak?" Tasha suggested. They stopped to consider the tree, which stood on their side of a wooden fence.

"You say that as if it's perfectly normal," said Briar.

"Isn't it?" Tasha asked, suppressing a giggle. "I mean, they grow all over the place."

"Look at the trunk on this one, the way it splits into two thinner trunks ending in branches with lacing smaller branches," Briar intoned like a tour guide. "Is it a confused oak tree, or a witch's hands with fingers twiddling?"

Tasha shook her head, laughing. "Don't freak me out," she said. She glanced at the tree again. "Shit! Now I can't stop seeing it!"

"Every time you see a split trunk, look for the witch's hands," said Briar.

"Where did you hear that?"

"I don't remember," said Briar. "But I guess it had to be my mom, when I was little. She used to tell me stories, ones she made up. Anyway, somebody also told me when the leaves fall in November, all the witches come out to play."

"With the beautiful, dead leaves," Gretchen said. "And—"

"With all of the dead children," said Orton.

"Anyway," said Briar. "I'm getting hungry. Are you?"

"I could eat," said Tasha.

"I can eat any time, anywhere," Briar told her. "Any amount of food."

"What are you doing tonight?" Tasha asked.

"The usual Saturday fun," said Briar. "Watching my mom get drunk with Ray."

"Call your landline," said Tasha. She handed Briar her phone. "Tell your mom you're spending the night at my house."

"She won't like it," said Briar.

"Come on," said Tasha. "You can eat dinner with us. It's chicken souvlaki night."

"Chicken souv-laki?"

"It's the only thing my mom can cook. She used to work at a Mediterranean restaurant when she was in college," said Tasha. "In the golden days of her wasted youth."

Briar dialed the number and waited. She flinched when Ray answered.

THE DAVIS
FAMILY

THEY MET in the foyer with the usual brief introductions, everyone on their best behavior. Tasha didn't have to warn her parents to mind their manners and check their sense of humor. They knew from the way she talked about Briar—the change to a conspiratorial tone, as though sharing a lifelong secret, and the conversational deference to her new friend—this was a special occasion. They were on trial and had better not blow it. Even so, they had a few awkward moments once the dinner was ready and they'd gathered around the table.

"*Briar?*" Charles repeated the name and smiled.

"Don't embarrass yourself," Kim told her husband.

Tasha rolled her eyes. "Forgive the parental antics," she told Briar. "They took a bonding class together before I was born, and they're still practicing."

"*Bonding?*" Briar asked with a grin.

"Zing!" said Charles.

"I told you they're weird," said Tasha.

"Oh, thanks very much," Kim said. She placed bowls of tzatziki sauce, olives, and salad on the table next to the plate of grilled chicken skewers.

"Briar," Charles said. "I apologize for our manners. Welcome to the Davis home. We're happy to meet you. Now, dig in."

They served themselves. Before each additional item she added to her plate, Briar hesitated. Urged to have as much as she wanted, she was obviously measuring each portion carefully, and pausing to see how Tasha ate her meal before taking a bite.

"I'm afraid it's a little fast-foodish," Kim said.

Briar swallowed and put down her fork before replying. "It's great, Mrs. Davis. It's delicious. Thanks for letting me stay over."

Tasha gave her friend a side-glance. Then she grinned and went on eating with gusto.

"We're glad to have you," said Charles. "I don't think we've hosted a visit from one of Tasha's playmates since…"

"Oh my god, Dad," Tasha mumbled with her mouth full.

"I guess that tells you how long it's been," he said.

"Relax, Dad," said Tasha. "We're not engaged or anything."

At this, Briar's eyes widened and she stifled a laugh. Then she lowered her gaze to her plate and went on eating.

"Well, I hope not!" Charles sputtered. When he realized what he had said, he added, "I mean, of course, there's nothing wrong with that. Except that you're fourteen and…"

"*Dad*," said Tasha. This prompted him to concentrate on his food for a while.

Kim's eyes were on Briar, taking in every word and gesture. Her voice was mild when she said to Tasha, "So, what's all of this about cutting class?"

"All of what?" Tasha asked.

"I had a call from school yesterday afternoon," Kim explained.

"Should we discuss it *now*?" Charles asked. "Over a meal?"

"I had cramps," Tasha said and then popped a forkful of chicken in her mouth.

Everyone else paused. Briar gave a little nod to Kim and Charles, confirming anything Tasha was about to tell them.

"Are you all right?" Kim asked her daughter.

"Fine," said Tasha. "It was no big deal. I felt sick, and I went to the bathroom instead of going to my last class. Briar helped me out. That's all. I sent you a text message to say I was okay, remember? Do we have to keep talking about this, Mom?" She gave a tiny nod toward her father, and Kim blushed.

"Sorry," Kim said. "I should have asked you about it last night."

"Great tzatziki," Charles said.

The decisive change of subject prompted a giggle from Briar. Tasha gave her a snarky grin.

"This is really good, Mrs. Davis," Briar said.

"Please," Kim told her. "Call me Kim."

"Thank you for having me, Kim," said Briar. And she beamed at them with all the admiration in the world.

* * *

Later that night, on her way to bed, Kim stopped by Tasha's room. The door was ajar and she pushed it open wider to say goodnight. When she saw the two girls, she froze. Both wore T-shirts and they were sitting upright with the covers pulled up around them, side-by-side in matching twin beds. With their heads turned toward her at the same angle they were, for one dizzying moment, nearly identical.

"Hi, Mom," said Tasha.

At this, Kim focused her attention on Tasha, now certain that the girl who was speaking was her daughter. "Hi," she replied. "Do you girls need anything? A bedtime snack?"

"After that meal?" Briar asked. She touched her tummy. "No way. That was amazing."

"Glass of water?" Kim asked. The girls shook their heads 'no.' "Um, tampons?"

"No, Mom," said Tasha, blushing. "We're fine. All good."

"Okay. Well, if you need anything during the night, I'm right down the hall."

Tasha nodded. "Thanks."

Kim slowly closed the door partway. After a second, she headed down the hall. Both girls sighed with relief. In perfect sync with one another, they dissolved into giggles and stifled their laughter with the bedclothes.

"Wow," said Briar once they recovered from their outburst. "You have a really nice family."

"They're okay," said Tasha.

"No," said Briar. "Your parents are great. They're the best."

"Yeah," Tasha admitted. "They're not bad."

"Hey," said Briar from across the divide. "Why do you have twin beds?"

Tasha stared at her with a grim expression and intoned, "I've been waiting for you."

Both broke out in giggles again. They put their hands over their mouths to stop.

"Sorry," Tasha said. "That was so weird."

"I don't care," Briar told her. "It's funny. Thanks for inviting me." She held out her hand between the beds, and Tasha reciprocated. When it was clear they couldn't reach one another, both mocked straining to touch fingers, grunting and dramatic, until they collapsed in another fit of laughter.

* * *

"What do you think?" Kim asked. She was rubbing lotion on her arms. Charles lay awake in bed, studying the ceiling as though he'd never seen it before.

"What do you mean?" he asked.

Kim shook her head. The strategies he used to avoid whatever subject she wanted to discuss could be exasperating.

48

"This girl," she said. "Briar. What do we know about her?"

"Nothing," he replied. "Everything. She's a lot like our daughter, same age, same school."

"Same terrible haircut."

"It's probably what they're all doing," he said.

"All of whom?" she asked.

"The girls at school," he said.

"No, they're not," she informed him. "And just because Tasha has a couple of superficial things in common with this girl—it doesn't mean anything."

Charles let out a sigh and rolled over to face his wife. He watched her climb into bed beside him. "If it doesn't mean anything, why are we here? Why bring our daughter to this place and send her to school with kids her age and encourage her to make friends, if none of it means anything? Isn't this exactly what we wanted—what you wanted?"

"No, no, no," Kim said. "Don't do that."

"I said, 'what we wanted.'"

"But you meant me," she said.

They lay facing one another in bed. Charles put his hand on her shoulder.

"Kim," he said. "It's all right. We're here and we're safe. Tasha has a real friend—which she hasn't had since third grade. It's natural to be a little cautious, but let's not wreck this for her."

"I would never," said Kim. "I want her to have all the things she needs."

"And," he said, "we have to understand, at some point—and we knew this would happen—we're not enough."

Kim grimaced, fighting tears.

"Kim."

"I know," she said. "I know."

"All right," he said gently.

"It's just..."

"What is it?" he asked.

"I don't..." she began.

"Spill," he told her."

"I'm not sure I like her."

"Oh, jeez," he said. "Come on."

"Isn't it possible Tasha doesn't know how to choose her friends?" she asked.

"Possible?" he asked. "Yeah. But you know that isn't what's going on."

"But it's possible she's making a mistake."

"Don't do this," he said.

"Allow for the possibility..." she began.

"No," he said. "No. Don't say these things. You're building a case against the only kid your daughter's brought home to meet us in literally years."

"But..."

"Can you hear it?" he asked, gently pointing a finger at her head. "The wheels are spinning, and you're trying to find a reason to scare Tasha away from someone she obviously likes and connects with, in that weird way that matters. It's chemistry."

"Is it?"

"And it's natural," he said. "It's natural for you to be a tiny bit jealous."

"I'm not," she said.

"Are you sure?"

"Maybe she's too young to choose without our help," said Kim.

"If that's true," he said, "then we've failed. This whole thing is a disaster, if what you're saying is true. Can you see that?"

They stared into one another's eyes. Charles brushed away a tear sliding down Kim's cheek. He cupped her face in his hand.

"Children grow up," he said. "This is inevitable. This is what it's all about. Parents teach kids how to live in the world so they can be happy and go about their own lives."

Kim shuddered. "What if she...?"

"Nothing terrible is going to happen," he said. "We know this, right? We've loved her and we've raised her to take an interest in things, and now all of our love is paying off. Can you see what I'm saying?"

Kim nodded. He brushed the strands of dark hair over her shoulder and kissed her.

"We have to let her find her way," he said.

"I can't let go," she said.

"You don't have to," he told her. "Just let her breathe. She'll always be your little girl, Kim. Let her breathe."

MRS. TED
VAN DEVERE

THEY'D BEEN at it for more than half an hour, and they were
louder than usual. The fence between the two trailers only ran along
the yard. At the front end a low hedge separated the adjoining lots,
and Mrs. Ted Van Devere could hear and see her neighbors dis-
tinctly.

Tonight's argument was about the girl, the woman's daughter,
who wasn't at home. The details came in fits and starts, thanks to
repetition.

The daughter had returned home late from school on the previous afternoon, which was bad enough. Now, according to the two
drunken parents discussing the matter, she was staying overnight
with a friend.

"What number was she calling from?" the woman yelled for
maybe the fourth time since the fight began.

"How would I know?" her husband or boyfriend yelled. "We
don't have callback, do we? I told you we should get callback. We
don't even know how many gigs I've missed because people called

and couldn't leave a message, and I didn't know their number and I didn't even know they called."

"What're you telling me?"

"Gigs," he yelled. "I'm losing jobs because of the phone!"

"It's your fault. You should get out there and give people your number."

"I should have a cell phone," he said.

"We should give *her* a phone," the mother wailed. "She deserves a phone! She's a girl. She needs a phone. What if she got stranded somewhere? How would she call us?"

"Pay telephone at the gas station," the man said.

"There're no pay telephone booths anymore! What are you talking about?"

"Well, she's not stranded," he said. "She's at a slumber party. Probably having a high old time. Bunch of little girls in their underwear showing each other their titties!"

"Shut up!" the woman screamed. "You shut up!"

"Don't get jealous, now," he said. "You're my girl, Evvy."

"Shut up and don't talk like that," she said.

"I'm just being funny," he said.

"You sell one of these goddamn guitars so we can buy a cell phone!"

"I'm working on that," he said. "You know I am!"

"What good is a goddamn landline?"

"Calm down, now," the man said. "Let me get you another beer."

"I don't want beer!" the woman wailed. "I want my baby! Where's my baby?"

"Okay," he said, holding out his hands to her.

"Where's my baby? Where's my baby?"

"Okay," he yelled. "Be quiet! Somebody's gonna call the cops!"

"I want my *baby*!" the woman screamed.

"Shut up!" he yelled, and slapped her.

Mrs. Van Devere flinched. Then she reached for the phone. She hated calling the authorities on a neighbor, but this was too much.

She wouldn't put up with a woman being beaten right in front of her. Then, to her astonishment, the woman threw her arms around the man and kissed him—a passionate, hungry kiss that continued as they staggered a bit, dropped to the sofa, and began tearing off their clothes.

"Oh, for crying out loud," said Mrs. Ted Van Devere. She put down the phone, turned out her living room light, and went to bed.

They were terrible parents. They were probably awful human beings. She fought the urge to judge, but this was a case of two people who should never have children.

She herself had never felt the inclination to give birth. The risk was unreasonable, knowing the number of malignant spirits out there seeking a vessel. Newborn infants were the most vulnerable. There were good reasons for all of the legends.

No, she preferred to pass her knowledge on to adolescent girls. Their will was strong, and if they were free of crime and cruelty, they made excellent students.

In the old days she would have taken the girl under her wing. She would have shown her how to make a root bag full of herbs and trinkets, to place under her pillow. She would have shared the secret to casting a spell using a lock of hair or fingernail clippings. Mrs. Van Devere was good at guessing character most of the time. She would be very surprised if the girl didn't have the gift. There was more at work in her head than the usual teenage drama, that was certain. Something marvelous emanated from her. Mrs. Van Devere hoped it could be turned to a natural purpose and not corrupted by the circumstances of her sad life.

Pointless pondering these things, Mrs. Van Devere decided. At the first sign of any connection between them, the girl's parents would have called the police. That's how people were nowadays. This was why women like Mrs. Van Devere had to keep to themselves. She had to be content with keeping the mobile home park safe from unnatural spirits that might lure the girl into something awful.

She closed her eyes and put on her sleep mask. In a minute the animal noises of her neighbors having sex would fade away, and her night's journey could begin. She wondered where she would go this time.

TASHA & BRIAR

TWO SETS of brown eyes peered over the top edge of the computer terminal. They tracked the progress of the school librarian, Mrs. Furillo, who was rolling a book cart up and down the stacks, returning volumes to the shelves. They'd been sent to work on a history paper, but their progress was hampered by lack of interest.

"Did you get detention?" Briar asked.

"No," said Tasha. "My mom signed a note telling the vice principal I had to leave early on Friday and forgot to ask permission. You?"

"I have to write an essay on the importance of education," said Briar. "If the VP doesn't like what I write, I'll have to do another assignment."

"Brutal. Can't your mom call the office and make an excuse?"

"My mom," said Briar, shaking her head. "She wasn't even there when I got home yesterday. Ray took her to the Sunday flea market to buy another guitar. Like he needs one. Then they went out to lunch at some diner. They showed up at about four o'clock and yelled at me for not letting them know where I was on Saturday."

"You called them," said Tasha. "They knew you were at my house."

"They were drunk on Saturday," said Briar. "When they're drunk they think everybody in the world is involved in a plot against them. They're crazy, Tasha."

"I'm sorry. Can't choose your parents, I guess. Isn't that a meme or something?"

"It's a curse," said Briar.

Tasha laughed. Then she remembered where she was and covered her mouth with her hand.

"Besides," said Briar, "Ray isn't my dad. He's just some rando loser my mom picked up in a bar."

From somewhere in the stacks came a sharp shushing sound. The girls surveyed the library checkout area and reference desk. They didn't see Mrs. Furillo, and they didn't see Tyler Blanchard sneaking up on them.

"Do you ever wonder about your real dad…?" Tasha asked Briar.

Tyler swung around behind the computer and slammed his hands on top of it. On one the faint imprint of teeth was still visible. He simpered, "Hey, don't worry, girls. I can give you what you need right here." He showed them a clenched fist.

"Get lost," Briar hissed.

"I need to vomit," said Tasha.

"Bulimic, Natasha?" he asked.

"Tyler Blanchard!" It was a mature woman's voice calling out, sharp and indignant.

Now it was Tyler's turn to jump. Mrs. Furillo had crept up behind him without making a sound until she shouted his name.

"Young man," she said. "Do you have school business with these young women? If not, please move along."

Tyler blushed, but he didn't turn red. The blood coursing beneath his pale skin flushed his neck and face purple. His head resembled a berry about to burst under pressure.

"Move *along*."

He obeyed the librarian without a word of apology. He strode across the main floor and shoved his way through the exit.

The girls sighed with relief. Mrs. Furillo went back to sorting and shelving books from her cart.

* * *

They met at the north end of the building after the last class of the day. They followed the same route they'd taken before, past Jessup's crumbling diner, except this time they skipped Curt Merritt's barn and continued on to the cottage with its garden full of birdhouses and windmills.

In the yard the girls settled on the wrought iron bench and watched a few tufts of cottonwood drifting in slow circles around them. The weather was mild. There was barely enough breeze to carry the soft white fibers through the air.

"What you asked me, at the library," Briar began. "About my real dad."

"Yeah?"

"My mom never talks about him," said Briar. "She doesn't have any pictures of him, or me. We don't have any family photos. Is that strange?"

"I don't know," Tasha said. "I guess so. My mom has a ton of pictures of me when I was a baby. They're funny, too."

"Why?"

"I guess I didn't grow any hair until I was two or three. I was completely bald and then, all of a sudden—big hair!" Tasha demonstrated with her fingers.

"At least you have some baby pictures," said Briar. She got up from the bench to examine the pile of gardening tools in the grass.

"Your mom didn't take any photos when you were born?" Tasha asked.

"Nope," said Briar. "I guess I wasn't all that photogenic."

They heard the garden gate creak behind them. Both girls turned to see Tyler approaching. Tasha jumped to her feet and automatically fished the phone out of her backpack.

"Aw," he said. "Now this is real sweet."

"Are you stalking us?" Tasha asked.

"You wish," said Tyler.

"You could only know where we are if you've been following us," said Tasha. "That makes you a stalker."

Briar was frozen where she stood. The gardening tools lay at her feet.

"If I'm a stalker," said Tyler, "you're a trespasser."

"The house is deserted," Tasha said, growing angry because she felt compelled to explain what they were doing. This was her special place, the only really beautiful thing she could share alone with Briar, and he was ruining it.

"Hey, bitch," he said to Briar. "Don't be shy. Come over here and let's finish what we started last week."

Tasha remembered the phone in her hand and held it up. "I'm calling my dad," she warned. "He'll kick your ass."

Before she could dial, Tyler stomped over one of the broken birdhouses on the ground between them. He slapped the phone from her hand and it went flying. He squared his shoulders and glared down at her.

"Now what're you gonna do?" he asked. His face was flushed purple, as though he'd been saving his rage for them since their last encounter in the library.

Tasha punched out at him and missed. Tyler grabbed her by the hair. She pulled to one side and he went with her. They fell in the grass, both struggling to remain upright. Tyler was grinning and wild-eyed. He shoved a hand inside Tasha's shirt. She felt his cold skin and the scrape of his fingernails. She bared her teeth and screamed and spat. She was reaching for his eyes when she heard a thud and Tyler released his grip on her.

They were both kneeling, breathing hard, clothes askew, and they remained so for a second. Then the expression faded from Tyler's face and he fell sideways onto the ground.

Tasha stared at his motionless body, then turned her gaze to Briar, who was standing over him with a block of wood in her hands. Both girls remained like this, stunned, silent, and uncertain what to do.

"Is he dead?" Briar asked.

Tasha leaned over Tyler and watched him. "No," she said, observing a small trail of saliva slipping from one corner of his mouth onto his chin. His chest was rising and falling. "He's hurt, but he's breathing. I don't know. He might be okay. I think he's okay."

Briar looked down at the piece of wood in her hands, and then dropped it. "There's no blood," she said.

"What should we do?" Tasha asked.

"Let's get out of here."

"Should we call 911?" Tasha asked.

"What for? He's alive. He doesn't deserve to be, but he's alive."

"Don't say that,' said Tasha. "He might have brain damage or something."

"How is that any worse than he was before?" Briar asked.

Tasha turned all of her attention to her friend, who was still watching Tyler with a kind of awed fascination. Every time he made a slight groaning noise, Briar's grin spread and her eyes grew brighter.

Tasha knew the thing to do was to seek help. But she weighed this knowledge against her fear for Briar, and for herself. What would happen to both of them if they called an ambulance? What they had done was self-defense. Tyler acted like an animal, stalking and attacking Tasha, and Briar had probably saved her life. She remembered the rough skin of Tyler's hand inside her clothes, groping her. He was a pig, and he deserved what happened to him. She knew it was wrong, but she hated him and she was glad he lay at her feet moaning. *Better him than us*, she decided.

They checked the ground and the bench for their belongings.

Tasha ran to the spot where her phone had landed. She made sure it was working and then slipped it into her backpack.

"Come on," she said to Briar. She stepped over Tyler and grabbed one of his arms. When a liquid gurgle rose from his throat, she dropped his arm in disgust. He was making a feeble attempt to turn his head, but the movement ended in a spasm. "Help me," Tasha said to Briar. "Let's leave him over there." She nodded toward the corner of the yard. "When he wakes up maybe he won't remember what happened."

They took hold of him by his shoulders. He was even heavier than they anticipated. They dragged him as far as they could, across the yard, lawn ornaments and birdhouses rolling away on either side of him, all the way to the side of the cottage. There they tossed dirt, leaves and weeds onto his arms and legs, to confuse the circumstances of his 'accident,' and because it felt right. He had disrespected them. He deserved to wake up in the middle of the night and wonder if he was dead or alive.

TASHA

THE WALK home wasn't long, but Tasha took her time. Her thoughts were jumbled, as if she were trying to awaken after a nightmare. Now that the adrenalin was fading she was beginning to question her actions. She kept trying to shake off the image of Tyler lying in the dirt and weeds.

She was sure he was alive, pretty sure he was all right. But what if he wasn't? They were only defending themselves against a creep who stalked them after school. She knew this was true, but she also knew what her dad would expect her to do.

They should have called for help. Now it was too late. If she ran back to the cottage and Tyler was awake, she would have to face him alone. If she called 911, they would record her number, and the fact that she had deserted an injured classmate. She wondered if she was violating some kind of Good Samaritan law.

The wind picked up and she pulled her sweater tight around her. Above and on the road, she could follow the currents of air by the white strands of cottonwood they carried. She tried to remember when the trees had shed their seeds in previous years. She couldn't recall seeing them so early in the spring, but her dad would know better than she. It was the kind of thing he loved to talk about over dinner—nothing personal, nothing dramatic; always the intricacies of the weather, or property values, or a new construction site in the area.

Before she reached the house, she spotted her mother. Kim was sipping a glass of wine and waiting, watching from inside the deck window, a maternal sentry on duty, dulling her paranoia and no doubt mumbling her latest relaxation mantra.

As Tasha crossed the lawn, she waved up at the deck. The gesture was casual, as always, calibrated to acknowledge Kim's presence without rewarding her for basically spying.

"Hi, mom," she called out in the foyer. "I'm home." She hoped her voice sounded normal. She placed her sweater on one of the wooden pegs in the hall and went upstairs to her room.

She knew Kim would wait for her in the massive concrete and wood living room, hoping for a full report of her day at school. But Tasha was tired of these little scenes where they both pretended to be excited about one another's lives, and she wasn't sure she'd calmed down enough to chat without revealing anything unusual. Kim might see through her and then the drilling would begin. Tasha feared she might even break down and tell her mom what had happened with Tyler. By now he was probably awake, had called his mom, had decided whether to tell the cops what the girls had done or keep it to himself.

He won't tell, she thought. *Tyler never changes*. Once, in second grade, she had tripped him when he passed her desk. He had flown through the air and crashed on the floor, but never breathed a word about Tasha.

"Hi," said Kim. She stood in the door to Tasha's room. She wore the conspiratorial expression that meant she craved 'girl time.' This might involve anything from re-reading *Sense and Sensibility* together to preparing Italian sodas from scratch. Tasha hoped it would be an easy wish to fulfill. At least Kim wasn't holding the glass of wine anymore. "I just had a great idea."

"Yeah?" Tasha was mortified by her inability to sound more excited. If she couldn't fake it, the conversation would take an emotional turn, with Kim trying more and more desperately to gain her full attention.

These days almost everything her mom suggested took the form of a mountain Tasha had to scale, a test to prove she wasn't drifting—or running—away. She sat through hours of morbid romantic movies and sliver-thin slices of cheesecake with chocolate sauce. She joined Kim for high tea at a fussy shop in Longview, eating cucumber sandwiches and gaudy pastries she could barely stand to swallow. She played navigator on their less and less frequent expeditions to Long Beach, where mother and daughter began their day with a visit to Jake the Alligator Man at Marsh's Free Museum. Kim would put a coin in the machine and a ruined penny would come out with Jake's image pressed into the copper. Then she would toss the coin in the air.

"Heads!" she would announce, inevitably, without showing the coin. "That means it's going to be a wonderful day."

Her mother just didn't get it. Tasha wasn't the nine-year-old who'd lived for these little adventures together. Her interests were changing, and nobody seemed to notice. She liked slow, meandering, nearly tuneless music these days, not the cheery pop tunes her mother preferred. She was developing a taste for stories by Thomas Ligotti and films by David Lynch, old masters of the psychological macabre. She'd long ago pushed the pink and fuchsia T-shirts and blouses to the back of her clothes closet, in favor of forest green and midnight blue. When Kim tried to talk her out of bobbing her long hair, Tasha had taken scissors to it herself.

"Why don't we take Briar out to lunch? Would that be fun?" Kim smiled.

"Sure, mom," said Tasha. She strained to think of something else she could offer. All she could picture was Tyler's face, purple with rage. "And, hey, thanks for the note. That was—cool. You got me out of detention."

Kim leaned back on her heels. Tasha thought it must take all of her self-control not to scream 'yay' at the top of her lungs.

It was horrible feeling bored when she was supposed to feel *something*, some tenderness. All of this was so much easier when she was little, when she wanted to be just like Kim. Over time she came to see her mother's shortcomings: her lack of close long-term friends, her failed ambition as an artist and how she had given up on that part of herself.

Now Tasha had the inkling, or a rising sense, of what it was like to be a woman in her own right. She wanted it. She craved it every time a decision was made for her—what film she would watch, how she would dress, who would be her best friend. This last was a more serious concern.

For the first four years of school, she'd been paired up with one girl after another on weekend play dates, an agreement made between mothers who wanted to maintain a certain social level for their children. As a result, by fourth grade Tasha had a reputation as the girl who needed her matchmaking mom to find friends. Some of the kids even spread the rumor that Kim had tried to pay a slightly older student to sit with Tasha during lunch and recess.

"No worries!" Kim said. "Let me know when you and Briar want to go out for lunch."

"Okay, I'll ask." Tasha nodded and kept on nodding while Kim backed out the door, still glowing from the tiny triumph of her 'cool' note to the vice principal. It was such a feeble victory it almost made Tasha want to cry.

BRIAR

GRETCHEN AND Orton stood beside the gate to the cottage garden. It was near twilight, and the vacant surrounding neighborhood was coming alive with insects and small nocturnal animals. An owl gave a premature *screech* from the woods.

Gretchen studied the scattered remains of lawn decorations and birdhouses. Orton sighed and shook his head.

"Told you," he said.

"What?" Gretchen asked.

"She's a bad one."

"They both did it," said Gretchen. "If you ask me, they're both bad."

"Nope," said Orton. "One's got the bad streak, and the other wants to play the hero."

"If you ask me, "Gretchen said again, "they both want to be heroes."

"Nobody asked you," said Orton. A crooked smile crept across his lips. He nodded in the direction of a dirt path that led to the gate where they waited. "See? Sure enough, here she comes."

Briar emerged from the darkening shadows and glanced around. When she was sure she was alone and unseen, she entered the yard by the gate, passing right between Orton and Gretchen. They stood by, unseen, while she stepped carefully among the debris and located the gardening tools. She isolated the shovel, pulled it free, and took a minute to breathe. Then she headed toward the spot along the side of the cottage.

Tyler lay where they'd left him. His chest was still rising and falling.

Once Briar determined that the dirt was soft and moist enough, she began to dig. It had been a long time since she'd worked this way, with the smell of grass and soil all around her. She thought of the bungalow in Tacoma where she'd spent all that she remembered of her childhood, and it seemed to her like a lost world: maple leaves shot through with scarlet in autumn, robins crying out in the spring when the magpies raided nests to feed their own young, and the gruff barking of the boxer next door whenever an ambulance siren started up in the night.

Briar made sure the hole was wide enough to accommodate Tyler's body, and just deep enough to discourage any wildlife casually scavenging for food. She plunged the shovel upright into the dirt to set it aside. Instead of the *chunk* of softened soil she heard a brittle *crack*.

Without a flashlight, she had to rely on scant moonlight beginning to spread across the yard. She crouched and stuck her hand in the dirt. She brushed it back and forth until she was able to feel and see something round, its contours both unfamiliar and unmistakable. Staring up at her from the center of the hole was a skull, bits of skin and hair still clinging to its rotten surface.

She fell back onto the grass and stared at the cottage. The brightness of its once-white walls and maroon trim, the whimsical birdhouses and windmills—it was all a lie, a mask protecting whoever had lived there from detection. Who would believe the person who lived in such a charming and silly home was a murderer?

"Ugh."

From where he lay on his back, covered in leaves and grass, with bits of cottonwood stuck to his face and clothes, Tyler was moaning. Briar watched him try to lift his head. Each attempt brought forth another guttural sound of futility. When she tired of the spectacle, she hoisted the shovel and brought the flat side down with a wet *crunch* on his face.

"There!" said Orton. He held out one arm and ushered Gretchen into the shadows. They crouched there together.

"Can she see us now?" Gretchen asked.

Orton nodded. "She can see lots of bad things now," he whispered.

When she finished burying her classmate, Briar sat on the grass for a few minutes, shivering. She didn't feel guilty, not really. She knew she had done the right thing. The next time Tasha visited her favorite place, it would be free of Tyler. He'd almost ruined it. This way, he would disappear and if Tasha didn't see any sign of him, if Briar managed to scatter enough debris to make the grave inconspicuous, after the next good rain it would be as if Tyler had never existed.

KIM

KIM HATED these conversations with her daughter. Inevitably, they left her feeling she had lost something. She had begged or cajoled instead of inviting. She had accepted pity instead of enthusiasm. She retreated to her office, a cozy room without windows, with only a small skylight above her desk, where she could concentrate on the dull work of pleasing clients online. This was also the space where she liked to hide away, to think things through.

What could she do? Tasha was a teenager, a fact Kim was still struggling to accept.

"What did you expect?" Charles had asked her recently. "Did you think she would never grow up?"

Of course Kim knew her daughter would change. She couldn't remain forever the tiny, messy, beautiful child gazing up with an adoring smile, but these vaguely unsettling prospects had been a distant glimmer in the future. She had been able to ignore the signs until Briar showed up. Now Tasha was best friends with a girl she barely knew, and Kim had to make the best of the situation. She had voiced her concerns and Charles had shrugged them off.

"We're safe," he had said. "You're not going to lose your child."

Was this true? Could she count on it? She had smiled and welcomed Briar into their home. She had complimented the girl on her tattoo of brown leaves, and her bizarre name. She was making plans to treat her to lunch, or maybe high tea. She was making sure all of her comments about Briar were positive. She was lying.

What Kim didn't say out loud was more personal and meaner than she wanted to admit: she didn't like Briar Kenny. There was something animal-like and strange about her. She seemed hungry, and not in the sense of having a healthy appetite. Some part of her soul was starving for attention.

Despite their obvious physical similarities, the girl had nothing in common with Tasha. She had nothing in common with any of them. She couldn't talk about movies or current events or her family and background. She upset the balance of the Davis household when she visited, even briefly. Worse, she reminded Kim of the sulky, slouching teenagers from her own youth.

At Tasha's age, Kim could have written a fat tome on the subject of female spite, every chapter the story of a different bitchy girl who alienated a mutual friend; invented a humiliating rumor; pretended to be pregnant long enough to gain the terrified attention of another girl's boyfriend; or went feral in public over a random, perceived slight.

Kim was aware of the influence hormones had played. They were girls coming into their own, wild children acting the way they thought adults behaved. They couldn't understand the consequences of the awful things they said and did, but she could never forgive all of these petty acts. At heart she agreed with the guidance counselor who'd once tried to comfort her with a blunt assessment: Adolescent girls were insane.

High school had been even more frightening. There, Kim had been surrounded by chronic bullies, older teens, usually beauties with the power to turn another girl into a pariah overnight. The worst of these were the former child models, of which there were a surprising number at Kim's affluent school. Instead of tattoos and piercings, they had nose jobs and bulimia.

Most of these young women had studied dance or acting at a local children's theater, and then moved on to model for Nordstrom catalogs and appear in TV ads. The really promising ones might speak a couple of lines of dialogue on an MTV series. They never went much further. Kim wondered what made them so grouchy—the perpetual dieting, or a sense of stalling out in high school? Maybe it was hard to retire and rest on your laurels at sixteen. Maybe they never got over it, early success curdling into a sense of failure when they contemplated the future.

Slender and tall with masses of dark brown hair, Kim never thought of herself as pretty. From the age of nine, she wanted to be a painter. She moved on from casual classroom projects to sketching and watercolor at eleven. Life drawing as a teenager made her a target of the Goth girls and former models.

She lived through it by holding fast to the conviction that she was special, an as-yet undiscovered artist with a lifetime of work ahead. She was years away from the crushing experiences of college, where all of her ambitions and accomplishments would come under the scrutiny of much older artists, all of them men, who would clarify how minor a talent she possessed and encourage her to take up interior decoration.

Anger and desire would carry her on through those years. She would graduate and set up a studio. She would move, with excruciating slowness and pain, from one gallery rejection to another, supporting her ambition waiting tables at a Mediterranean restaurant on Capitol Hill.

She couldn't measure the infinitely small increments of loss. She was haunted by the idea that she might have done much better with only a tiny dose of encouragement.

Kim assumed things were better for kids these days. She read the newsletters and bulletins from Tasha's school. She was convinced that teachers were more aware than they used to be. Girls were encouraged to develop self-esteem. Boys were allowed to be thoughtful and sensitive. Clark Middle School students were expected to treat one another with respect. Hazing was forbidden by the administration. But how could they know all of the ways in which kids could torment one another?

It had been a slap, a throwback to a scary time in her life, on the Saturday afternoon when Tasha dragged her new best friend home. Instantly Kim was unnerved by the sly grin and raccoon eye makeup, a look Tasha imitated immediately, in a modified fashion. In all other respects, standing side-by-side, the two girls appeared to mirror one another, with their heads inclined together and one hand (Briar's right, Tasha's left) resting on a hip. Together like this, without trying, they formed a three-dimensional Rorschach, an inkblot in the rough shape of a heart.

Dinner had been awful. Briar was an intruder, a girl so deprived she thought souvlaki was a delicacy. She resembled a stray cat suddenly introduced to canned meat and a bed by the fire.

Kim had felt a stabbing irritation all that evening, a wish to strike out. The expression 'wrong side of the tracks' came to mind. But she had remained calm. She'd served dinner and smiled and asked questions, feigning interest in Tasha's playmate.

"What do your parents do?"

"Mom," Tasha had chided. "Please."

Kim had sat there, gutted. How was it possible for her daughter to find this scruffy girl fascinating? What role was Kim supposed to play now? Should she explain why Briar wasn't a suitable friend, or was it better if she pretended not to care? All of this felt like a test, but which kind? Was it a measure of her maternal concern, or her coolness?

The new buddy had slipped away from her scrutiny at one point during the evening and slouched in a corner of the kitchen, coming to rest and leaning against a wall as though she had good reason to be exhausted. She was a bony, tall girl clutching the ends of her sleeves in pale hands with grimy fingertips. She looked disheveled and uncoordinated in loose-fitting black jeans, a brown jersey, and scuffed ankle boots. Worse was the tangle of dead ivy and brown leaves tattooed on the left side of her throat. Kim would later learn from Tasha, who was too cool to ask before Briar offered the information, that the tattoo was an ill-conceived tribute to a young singer's last album before he committed suicide. Who would let her daughter compromise part of her body, her skin, for such an ugly thing?

Aside from these gripes about attitude and appearance, and the way they reminded her of girls long gone from her life, Kim couldn't put her finger on the source of her unease. There was nothing else overtly wrong with Briar, aside from being awkward.

Above her desk, the skylight framed a darkening sky. Bits of fluff drifted through the air. She couldn't remember what it was called, the tree that shed its seed attached to these white strands. It was something obvious, but it kept eluding her.

No matter what, Kim intended to make the best of the situation. If she didn't overreact, the girls would naturally grow tired of one another. She told herself Briar wasn't a dangerous influence, just a lonely teenager thrown into an awful situation purely because of bad choices made by the adults in her life.

And who were these adults? Kim didn't know the mother or the stepfather. She had never seen them around town, or shopping, or at the occasional school event. Her Facebook search had turned up a page for Rayburn J. Kenny - Musician. In the profile photo a rangy, middle-aged man in jeans, an embroidered shirt, and cowboy hat held a guitar. He looked like every backup player in every cheap club Kim had ever visited as a college student. His most recent post—bragging about a gig in Olympia—was three years old.

She knew nothing more about the Kenny family, and so, aside from a strange tattoo, why did she assume their choices were destructive? She had a strongly negative impression of these people who could only afford a trailer park rental in Skillute. What had they done, when they were younger, to end up so impoverished?

According to Tasha's brief conversations with Charles, these were parents who made their teenage daughter sleep on a sofa bed in the living room. Were they gamblers or drug users? Kim wanted to forbid her daughter to visit their home, but she knew this was exactly the challenge a teenager would relish. She had to bide her time for the friendship to fade, while imagining a drunken guitar player sprawled on a sofa—his stepdaughter's bed—with no pants on.

These thoughts brought a wave of something akin to pity for Briar, and Kim couldn't afford sympathy. She desperately wanted to break this hold the girl had on her daughter, but she couldn't appear to do so.

The information on Rayburn Kenny's Facebook profile was out of date. Kim typed his name and performed a quick Google search. At least he wasn't in hiding. His phone number, with a Skillute area code, turned up immediately.

BRIAR

SHE WALKED home as quickly as she could, sticking to the one route she knew through the sparsely populated woods and across overgrown vacant lots. She'd started the day in a foul mood and ended with—well, she wasn't sure what to call it. Now she was experiencing something odd, considering what they'd done to Tyler. Her initial fear had been replaced by something much easier to bear. She felt elated. She breathed in the fragrant night air of spring and knew she had done the right thing, no matter what anyone else might think.

It was getting late when she opened the front door, and she was shocked to find Evelyn on the telephone. Excuses she might offer ran through her mind. She prayed her mother wasn't calling the police out of worry. This was unlikely. Evelyn had never called the cops, not even on the night a prowler broke the back lock on their place in Tacoma. She taught Briar to understand that the authorities were trouble, and ordinary people were better off settling their disputes and problems on their own.

"Well, like I say," Evelyn explained to the person on the phone.

"It might be okay." She rolled her eyes at Ray, who was sitting on the sofa in his underwear applying some kind of polish to a banged-up guitar. "Oh, I'm sure she would have a good time. But I've got to look at our plans for the week and see if she can make it."

Briar froze. There wasn't anyone else Evelyn could be talking about.

"Well, give me your number and I'll let you know as soon as I can," Evelyn said. "Mm-hm." She listened to the person at the other end, but she wasn't writing anything down. "Sure," she said. "Enjoy what's left of your evening." She hung up and turned to Ray.

"Who was it?" he asked.

"One of Briar's new stuck-up friends."

"Who was it?" Briar asked. "What did you say?"

"You heard me," said Evelyn. "I said I'd have to see."

"About what? See about what?"

"Well, look at you, all excited over a phone call," said Ray. "You got a boyfriend?"

"Shut up," said Briar. She turned to her mother. "Who was it?" When Evelyn smiled at Ray, Briar shoved her. Ray shambled to his feet.

"You don't touch your mom," he said. The fumes from the polish rose with him. He had a couple of stains of it on his undershirt.

"I've told you about a million times," Evelyn said. "You don't run off with people. You don't go anywhere without telling me first."

"When have I?" Briar tried to control her voice. If she shouted or lashed out again, things would be much worse.

"Just this past weekend," said Evelyn. She plopped down on the armchair.

Taking his cue from her, Ray sat on the sofa again and went back to ruining the guitar with what Briar assumed was the wrong kind of polish. Everything he did was wrong.

"I called you," said Briar. "I told Ray where I was. I gave him the phone number and the address. I can't help it if your boyfriend is too stupid to write a message."

"You don't talk to him like that," Evelyn warned.

"I wasn't talking to him," Briar said.

"Well, that's it," said Evelyn. "You're grounded. So you can tell your friend's mom you won't be going out to whatever it is—tea or something. No, wait. You can't tell her. I'm going to tell her."

"Where does she want me to go?" Briar asked. She kept her voice in check but it was a strain. She was fighting the urge to cry.

"Oh, now you wish you'd been nicer to me," said Evelyn. She got up and went to the fridge for beers. She handed one to Ray on her way back. "Too late, miss. I'm going to tell that stuck-up bitch you're grounded for the rest of the school year."

Ray chuckled. Briar stood staring at her mother, and she felt her breath go shallow. "What's her number?" she asked.

Evelyn met her gaze.

"What's the number?" Briar asked again. "You didn't write it down. Where does she live? What's her name?"

"Maybe I've got it all memorized," said Evelyn.

"Right," said Briar. "Right." She stomped out the front door and slammed it shut after.

She could hear them, 'Evvy' and 'Ray-Ray,' laughing. She knew what they would do next.

It was the same every night. Evelyn came home from her shift at the dog groomer's. She found Ray plucking mindlessly at his guitar or, like today, pretending to do something useful. They would decide to reward their hard work with a 12-pack of cheap beer and a couple of joints. They would listen to music—lousy, stupid, loud music. And after guzzling all they could hold and eating all the leftovers in the fridge, they would start talking dirty to one another and stumble off to the bedroom, leaving Briar to clean up the kitchen, eat dinner scraps, and set up the sofa bed.

She would lie awake in the dark, sometimes crying and sometimes thinking of running away. She would only fall asleep every night when she heard both of them snoring.

* * *

Briar walked around the side of the trailer. The air was cool, with an almost imperceptible breeze. Despite the hour, Mrs. Dead Lavender was puttering in her garden, pulling weeds, illuminated by a glass lantern hung on a pole.

Ordinarily Briar would have avoided the old woman. Tonight she didn't have the energy. She sat down on a broken-down lawn chair, pulled a joint from her pocket, and lit up.

Mrs. Dead Lavender crept closer to the cedar fence that divided the back end of their adjoining lots. She placed a slender, heavily veined hand on top and said, "You mind if I take a toke?"

Briar got up and went to the fence. She hesitated. Then she exhaled to one side, and handed the old woman the joint. To her surprise Mrs. Dead Lavender pinched it expertly, inhaled deeply, and closed her eyes. They stood together and passed the joint a couple of times.

"I hope you don't mind an observation," said the old woman. Her eyes were light gray, almost silver in the faint glow of the lantern. "Your parents aren't very nice people."

Briar laughed bitterly. She shook her head. "Ray's a jerk," she said. "My mom wasn't this bad until she met him, Mrs. Dead..." She almost called the woman by her nickname but stopped herself.

"That's all right," said the woman. "I've been called plenty of names. I'm sure the one you've made up isn't the worst."

Briar felt a chill. She wasn't ashamed, just uneasy about having her thoughts and actions guessed at by a stranger. She wondered how much the old woman knew. She made an effort to put Tyler out of her thoughts. She did this by concentrating on the Davis family and how much she wanted to be like them.

"Mrs. Ted Van Devere is a false name, too," the woman told her.

"What's your real one?" Briar asked, and wondered if she was being brassy again. Ray was constantly telling her what she lacked in looks and brains, she made up for in brass.

"If I told you my real name," the old woman said, "I'd have to turn you into a toad."

Briar laughed. "Can you turn Ray into a toad?"

Mrs. Dead Lavender smiled. "You're going to be all right," she said. "People survive all sorts of awful things. Especially women, we're much stronger than anyone thinks. We're not defined by other people unless we want to be. Try to remember that." She handed Briar the depleted roach and returned to her night gardening.

Briar could hear Ray and Evelyn laughing drunkenly in the Kenny trailer. When their voices grew softer, she knew they had retreated to the bedroom. She gazed up. The sky was cloudless, black, shimmering with endless stars.

She had done what she had to do, for Tasha's sake. She didn't see why she couldn't do the same for her own sake. Even Mrs. Dead Lavender could tell how crummy Ray was. In his way, he was as bad as Tyler. In fact, he was worse. He had invaded their lives and wrecked everything. There was no new house under renovation. The guitars cluttering their home were junk he was never going to repair.

Briar studied the sky. She thought about a world without the Tylers and the Rays, and the idea made her smile.

MRS. TED VAN DEVERE

SHE WAS floating. Her mind lifted her up, cloudlike and phosphorescent, over the mobile home park. She knew the patches of fir and pine trees, once a dense forest covering the entire town of Skillute and beyond, now cut back to mere shade flanking a dozen narrow walking trails.

Here and there, lots had been cleared and sectioned off but never developed. On some of these lots the foundation for a house had been laid. On others, construction had stalled after a frame was erected. The incomplete homes weathered season after season, wood rotting, the surrounding grass growing wild with weeds and scraggly flowers.

She hovered in the cool night air above her friend Odelia Farrow's old cottage. The house remained sturdy but the garden lay in disrepair, the wooden windmills and birdhouses broken and tangled with vines. She couldn't see inside the cottage and only vaguely sensed the presence of someone, alive or dead, in the shadows.

A breeze lifted, and carried her on to the site where Beverly

Dempsey's home once stood. Burned to the ground years before with two women inside, the land had been cleared and leveled, expanded beyond the former edge of the forest. The house occupying the spot now was much finer than Beverly's. A spacious two-story with floor-to-ceiling windows and a wraparound cedar deck displayed the prosperity of its owners, a couple named Davis with a teenage daughter.

Nothing in this home was what it seemed. The Davises had spent their years in Skillute hiding from the cruelties of the world, unaware that they shared meals with silent silhouettes and slept in the company of pale monsters.

Mrs. Ted Van Devere could hear the family, breathing and talking in their sleep. They were troubled and they didn't know why. In their own dreams they traversed the ravaged woods and climbed the jagged hillsides, all without realizing they were bridled and urged on by mischievous spirits. When they awoke each day, they felt more tired than the night before.

She would have drifted on and on from house to house, as she liked to do, but she was drawn back by the sound of crackling timber. She heard rattling glass and metal. Joists gave way and sank into flames. Worst of all was the scent, the ancient and unmistakable combination of smoke and flesh.

She sat up in bed and removed the sleep mask from her eyes. At once the room grew brighter. Flickering orange fingers of light shuddered against the walls.

She knew as soon as she reached the window that the fire wasn't in her own home, but the one next door. She saw flames shooting from the windows and the front door of the Kenny trailer. She heard wood snapping and splitting. Through the billowing smoke, she could barely make out the shapes of two people standing on the lawn before she reached for the phone.

* * *

The next day Mrs. Ted Van Devere read about herself and the Kenny family in the local paper. She realized she had made a mistake talking with the girl. She had missed something crucial, and she couldn't rest until she knew what it was.

* * *

At two a.m., a senior resident at the Maplewood Mobile Home Park had dialed 911 and reported a fire at the trailer next door. Firefighters and EMTs arrived to find a middle-aged woman and a teenaged girl standing on the gravel driveway, a few feet apart from one another, silently watching the blaze.

The woman and the girl said nothing while firefighters worked to contain the conflagration. They allowed EMTs to move them to a medical vehicle and check their vital signs. They appeared to be in shock, both of them wearing nightclothes that were lightly singed, their faces streaked from smoke and sweat.

It was when the medics brought out a stretcher bearing the covered remains of Rayburn Kenny that Evelyn Gamel began to scream. She rushed toward the stretcher and had to be held back. She fell to the ground, in the gravel, while neighbors looked on. And when the police officers asked her what she could tell them, she said, "I killed him. I killed my husband. It was me, I killed him."

Young Briar had little to say to the police about her stepfather's demise. Her version of events was straightforward but lacking detail: Ray was polishing a guitar that night. He'd had a lot to drink. Her mother woke her up and helped her outside. The rest was confusing.

Evelyn might have been arrested on a charge of manslaughter if she hadn't confessed to killing her boyfriend, whom she persisted in referring to as her husband. She was taken into custody and remanded to county jail, pending a psychological evaluation.

Briar was a minor with no other relatives nearby. Her loudly stated wish was to move in immediately with her friend Tasha Davis.

"I'm afraid that's not how we do things," a female police officer explained. "We have to get you to a safe place, and then a social worker will make inquiries and determine how to proceed."

"I know how to proceed," Briar said. "My friend's family wants me to move in. Call and ask if they can pick me up."

"You've been through a lot," said the police officer. "You might be confused right now, but trust me, you're safe."

Briar was allowed to call her friend Tasha. Soon after this, she was escorted by a social worker to the nearest care facility approved by the state, a local shelter that had once been the home of a preacher and his wife. There she was counseled briefly by an assigned social worker and a child psychologist, handed a Bible and a brightly illustrated pamphlet on the subject of grieving, and told not to worry, things would get better.

THE DAVIS
FAMILY

STANDING BEFORE her parents, who sat attentively on the living room sectional, Tasha recounted the gruesome details of Briar's ordeal with tears welling, her voice wavering. She added quite a lot to what Briar had told her on the phone, conjuring a scene of carnage and mayhem, a poor girl stranded all alone in a dangerous world, standing on the lawn and staring at the charred remnants of her home. Worse, her family had been obliterated: A stepfather burned alive before her eyes and a mother gone mad and taken into custody. Tasha pleaded with her parents as fervently as she'd once begged to keep a three-legged cat that followed her home.

"Why can't Briar just stay with us until the end of the school year? It's hardly any time at all. We have plenty of space. She can share my room. It's perfect."

Defying every natural impulse, the Davises regarded their daughter calmly. They were following an objective strategy they'd decided upon years ago: *Never appear to panic. Remain centered. Breathe normally.*

"Your classmate is a minor," said Charles in the balanced, civil tone Kim referred to as his 'fatherly voice.' "So this isn't our call. It's up to the county to say where she stays and for how long, if her extended family can't make arrangements."

Tasha stared at him in disbelief. "She's not a 'classmate.' She doesn't need 'arrangements.' She's my friend. She ate with us. She slept here. And if you offer to help and explain that we already know her..." Tasha begged.

"What do we really know?" Kim asked. "I mean, you just met her last week, didn't you?"

"I can't believe this," Tasha said. "It's...this is, like, the opposite of everything you ever taught me. Why are you acting like this?"

"Doesn't she have *any* relatives nearby?" Kim asked.

"If she did, if she had family nearby, why would she be stuck in a shelter? Why?" Tasha pulled an expression her mother was getting to know well, a sideways glance with a quick sigh of exasperation.

"I think it's a very nice place, where she's staying," Charles said. "If it's the place I'm thinking of, it's a big residential house someone donated to the town, for the temporary care of people in situations like this."

"Situations like this?" Tasha asked.

"For people in need."

"Look, Dad," said Tasha. "Briar's real father disappeared when she was little. She doesn't even remember him. All of her grandparents are dead. Her stepdad wasn't really married to her mom, and his family doesn't want her. If we don't help soon, she might have to go into foster care with *strangers*. Think about that. It's horrible. And it would be all your fault."

Tasha paused and let the weight of her words sink in. A smudge of mascara underscored both of her brown eyes. It was a style she'd picked up from Briar, along with loose-fitting jeans and messy sweaters. She was almost as sloppily dressed and over-made-up as the tiny girl who used to pick the lock on her mother's vanity table and play runway model with lipstick and rouge.

The child she used to be was only a few years behind them, yet Tasha seemed to have forgotten her. Forgotten, lost, or buried at some unacknowledged point. Who knew if she would ever return? Meanwhile, the fourteen-year-old standing before her parents was becoming, bit-by-bit each day, someone they barely recognized.

"We'll talk it over," Charles said.

Kim turned to him with a shocked expression.

"Please, Dad," said Tasha.

"Everything will be okay," Charles said quietly. "Don't worry."

* * *

Even at night the cottonwood strands drifted through the air, landing in rough, woolly batches on the foothills and sparse forests of Skillute. Kim could see them wandering the night sky, framed by a window against the far wall. When Tasha was a little girl she used to stand on the lawn with her head tilted back, watching the annual shedding of seed, her eyes sparkling with delight. She called the white fibers of the cottonwood 'witches.' She followed their progress and chased them with a butterfly net. For years, Kim could make her laugh by mentioning the 'batches of witches' they used to catch and keep in a jar.

Husband and wife lay awake in bed with the lights on. Both were groggy from too much Pinot Noir.

"You can't be serious," Kim whispered. "Tell me you're not really considering this."

"What else can we do?" Charles asked.

"We can say no."

"How?" he asked. "How do we explain it, if we say no?"

"We know nothing about this girl," Kim said.

Charles studied her face. "And she knows nothing about us," he said. "Kim. We can afford to be generous here. Take her in with the stipulation that she can only stay long enough to finish out the school year. After that, other arrangements have to be made. We look like heroes to Tasha, and there's no harm done."

"No harm," Kim said. "Anything could happen."

"All right," he said. "And what do you think will happen if we refuse?"

"Tasha will get over it," Kim told him. "The way she got over that hideous cat when she was nine years old."

"What if she doesn't? Think about it, Kim. She dragged home that dying cat and let it sleep on her bed right after you suggested getting rid of the second twin bed. Remember? You told Tasha she could redecorate her room and she could have a canopy bed and a vanity and a sofa. What did she say?"

"She told me the second twin bed still belonged to 'Tilly,' even if she had gone away," said Kim. "And if she ever came back, she wouldn't have a place to sleep."

"And what did you say?" Charles prompted.

"I told her it was time to let her imaginary friend go."

"The next day," Charles reminded her, "she brought home a three-legged cat, carried it into the living room, and announced that it was going to live here forever."

"Shedding fur all over the house."

"She said if the cat couldn't stay, she was leaving too," said Charles.

"Why do you have to bring this up?" Kim asked. "It isn't the same thing."

"It's the same," said Charles. "You know it's the same, and you know why. It was the same when the cat—disappeared."

"It had mange," Kim said. The corner of her mouth curled in disgust. "Its teeth were falling out."

"When Tasha came home from school and it was gone, she was inconsolable."

"Charles, it isn't the same thing. It can't be."

"Inconsolable," he said. "Until we told her she could keep the twin beds as long as she wanted. Nothing would change. We would live here, and her room would stay the same. And if Tilly ever came back, she would be Tasha's sister and live with us forever. That's what we promised."

"She was nine years old," Kim said. "She's a teenager now."

"A teenager who's never redecorated her room. A teenager with twin beds, who dragged home a girl who had no friends, and asked us to take her in."

"But what can we do?" Kim asked.

"Take her in," said Charles. "Be good parents, and let our daughter have what she needs."

"Forever?" Kim asked.

"She doesn't expect that," Charles assured her. "She only expects us to be kind to her friend."

Kim sighed heavily. Through the window behind Charles she could see the cottonwood floating against the night sky, thick and drowsy as spring snow. Since she had remembered the name it seemed to be everywhere, all the time.

"Only until the end of the school year," she said. "Then Briar has to go."

* * *

Alone in her room, Tasha lay on her side. She stared at the empty twin bed next to her own and wondered what more she could do to help Briar. Now they were more than best friends. What they had done to Tyler locked them together in secrecy.

There were stories in the news about the fire and Evelyn Kenny's confession, but nothing about a missing teenager. Had Tyler stumbled home, or had someone found him and called an ambulance? Tasha checked the news online hourly, and although she shared her parents' religious skepticism, she said a silent prayer for Briar's safety.

KIM

KIM AND Charles met two months after she graduated from college. He was a year ahead of her, and it made a difference in terms of their expectations. He'd spent twelve months earning a decent salary as a project manager for a property development company. In comparison, she was still thinking like a student, determined to prove her university art professors wrong by showing her work at galleries around Seattle and selling her paintings to collectors.

Back then, she had the youthful will and the stamina to trudge uphill on Denny and Queen Anne, across Beacon Hill and Georgetown, hauling her portfolio. She stood in line for three hours, only to be judged unworthy of the Cascadia Biennial exhibition. She knew she was struggling, but she didn't mind. She was painting. She was an artist. Success would come, she believed.

They met at a bus stop in a rainstorm. The bus was late. Charles gallantly offered to share his umbrella, but as soon as Kim stepped underneath it, the wind flipped it inside out and carried it off down the street.

Their first date was coffee at Bauhaus. Kim was sly about choosing a table directly under one of her own works, the first to be displayed in public and the only one in the café not bearing a SOLD sign.

Charles had spent five minutes trying to explain what he did for a living. Kim found it too tedious to follow, but she loved his self-deprecating stories. All of them ended with him in a muddle over some miscommunication with his boss.

"What do you think of this?" she asked, pointing to the canvas on the wall above.

Charles studied the painting, taking his time. He seemed to want to take it all in before making an evaluation. At last he cleared his throat and said, "I don't think I've ever fallen in love with a non-representational work of art before, but this is fierce and—I don't mean this in a negative way—kind of crazy. I like it."

Years later Kim would continue to wonder if she had kissed him then because she loved his words, or the way he spoke, or the tenderness of his eyes, or simply the fact that he recognized her when no one else did.

* * *

The first year Kim and Charles lived together, all of their differences became apparent. "Like bloodstains on a white carpet," Kim's mother used to say.

Kim ignored the differences in their nature. She wanted Charles so badly and she wanted this to work. By the end of their first year she had become expert at preparing one dish, souvlaki; had sold her painting from the café for three hundred dollars; and had mastered the art of postponing the inevitable.

Charles wanted to start a family.

"I'm not saying I don't like the *idea* of a family," she said one night over a bedtime glass of Burgundy. They had been together fourteen months, and Charles was starting to drop hints at every opportunity. He lay sprawled across the bed, facedown, his feet dangling over the edge, saying nothing. "I'm only pointing out that we have plenty of time."

She yearned to go further, to have a real conversation on the subject, to talk openly about her reservations, but she was afraid. He spoke of their future family as a given, an inevitability. Kim couldn't imagine her future without Charles, but she could easily imagine it without children. She wondered what would happen to her work—back then, she still thought of making art as her work—when a baby came along. Could she fit a playpen and a baby-sized swing set into her already cramped studio? Where would the baby sleep? How many hours a day would be devoted to childcare, and how many to painting? When would Kim be free to do whatever she wanted?

"We do have plenty of time," said Charles. He sat up and took a swig of wine. "And we don't. We might never be as well-equipped as we are now to create a healthy family. The other day I was reading an article about fertility and male hormones…"

He could go on like this for hours. He could talk for the sake of talking, discuss for the sake of discussion. This was never the habit in Kim's family, where both men and women could be taciturn to the point of incivility. She had an uncle who was stabbed in the arm by his girlfriend for failing to answer the question, "Where should we dine tonight?"

"You've said yourself," Charles continued, "most marital breakups are over money or children. One person wants kids and the other doesn't, but no one really discusses the subject until it's too late. We're so lucky. We're in agreement about this fundamental thing. I want to enjoy every moment of whatever time we have together with our children. Do you understand what I'm saying? I feel like we're missing out every day on this powerful, *majestic* experience." He leaned across the bed and kissed her. She lied and said she knew exactly what he meant.

"I love kids, I really do," she said, which was a ridiculous exaggeration. "Except for the lousy ones, of course."

He laughed. "Lousy?"

"The ones who turn out badly," she said, realizing she was on shaky ground. "Or the ones who are so difficult, nobody can do anything with them."

"Difficult?"

"Remember the *New York Times* piece about adoptive parents who can't cope," she said. "So they give the children back, or give them away? That one woman, she spent a fortune to become an adoptive single mom. When the whole thing went south, she killed the boy she adopted...?"

"Oh, no, no," he said. "Let's not dwell on these stories, Kim, please. They're creepy."

"They're real news articles, not stories. These things happen. People find out, after a while they realize, that they don't love their children. And they can't stand knowing it. They can't cope."

"When you focus on these terrible stories, they build up in your imagination," he said. "They grow. They fester. They poison people's minds against children who need help. Besides, we're not adopting. Our kids will be like us, and we'll adore them."

It was Kim's greatest fear, and he would never understand. What if she simply couldn't cope, or what if she didn't like their child? The thought was constantly nagging her. Who didn't love babies and children? Who didn't want a precious, tiny duplicate of themselves to spoil?

If Kim could have been completely honest, without fear of losing Charles, she'd never been very interested in motherhood, either the role or the subject. But when Charles talked about how cute and funny a friend's child was, Kim nodded and smiled, her thoughts drifting away to a new project or dinner plans or the weekend.

She continued working part-time at a Mediterranean restaurant where she had earned rent while she was in school. The owner was a beloved matriarch, an affectionate mother and grandmother, as well as a successful entrepreneur. She liked to say she had created a business by feeding her family with love.

A generous section of the dining area had been converted to a playroom, with barely discernible boundaries. The idea was to let kids be kids while their parents enjoyed a delicious platter of chilled oysters or a dish of marinated feta.

Almost without exception, the dining parents viewed the children's area as a free-babysitting zone. From the moment they entered the dimly lit, delightfully fragrant interior of the restaurant, they released all obligation to mind the activities of their offspring. The kids ran wild, smearing the walls with crayon, screaming at one another, racing back and forth to the kitchen door, tripping up the waitresses and hurling bits of pita bread across the room.

Kim could never get over it. She expected single people and unmarried couples—the 'non-parentals,' as Charles called them—to quit coming in, but they seemed to get a kick out of the children and the noise. Maybe they thought of it as practice for parenthood, or a really rowdy lounge act, or maybe they just didn't mind tzatziki in their hair as much as Kim did.

In the earlier days of their relationship, she'd recounted all of these awful incidents to Charles. When she described stepping on a lemon wedge dropped by a toddler in the dining area and skidding against a table, he chuckled. When she told him about Little Princess, a staff favorite who wore a Disney ballroom gown and smacked other kids in the face with her scepter, his expression turned wistful. When she mentioned a four-year-old boy who greeted customers and waitresses by ramming them in the abdomen with his head, Charles merely speculated that the boy might make "a hell of a linebacker someday."

After a while, she stopped telling him how her shift had gone. It was a waste of time. Charles had a theoretical family living in his head, an *Eight is Enough* brood, while her imagination tended toward the Cronenberg variety. No amount of real-life evidence would ruin his fantasy. For a while, Kim even tried inviting him to the restaurant for a bite to eat before and after her shifts, vainly hoping the experience might put a damper on his enthusiasm.

"Look at *this* guy," he would say, and laugh, pointing at a chubby toddler whose onesie was soaked in iced tea. "He kills me!"

"Yeah, he kills me too," she replied, wishing she had the nerve to point out the mess to his oblivious mom and dad.

* * *

A year and a half into their life together, they married. Just a civil ceremony, 'to get it over with,' as Kim saw it, the getting married part a mere technicality in the ongoing story of her love for Charles.

He was still hungry for a family. This was apparent in every decision he made. Each proposed move, from studio to one-bedroom to two-bedroom apartment, sent him dashing to his laptop to investigate the available schools. One thing he was adamant about was public education. He was convinced that private schools limited children socially. He wanted a family with no biases about money and class. Less obviously, yet quietly underscoring conversations with friends and co-workers, Charles expressed his desire for Kim to want a family as much as he did.

"Parenting is a team sport," he said one night, in all seriousness, to a guy who played drums for a terrible grunge tribute band Charles and Kim followed.

The guy nodded too many times and said, "Yeah, you know it is."

"She'll get there," everyone reassured Charles. "She'll come around. She's young. Don't worry about it, not yet anyway. Wait another year and you'll see." Sometimes they said these things right in front of her.

It was as if they all thought something was broken or malfunctioning inside her. She was a mechanism, an appliance with faulty wiring or bad timing, but she could be repaired. Given love, and patience with her strange nature, she would want what all women wanted. One day her body would demand it, and she wouldn't have to think about it anymore.

* * *

Of course her baby was perfect. She arrived on time and at a convenient hour, mid-morning. One of the nurses told Kim she'd never seen a smoother, less difficult birth, and relayed this to everyone on the maternity ward.

"Textbook delivery," the nurse said. Kim tried to summon up the bile to vomit on her.

Then came the deluge of phone calls, text messages, stuffed animals, blankets (as if she didn't have enough from the shower a month earlier), and visits from friends who turned into sniveling idiots when they saw what Kim and Charles had created. No one could get over how contented the infant seemed.

"Smug," said Kim out loud one afternoon. This was after the hoopla had given way to long days alone, stranded at home with the baby. She stared down at her daughter, who was buckled into her sleeper and swaddled in a yellow blanket. "You smug thing," she said to the baby. "You don't have to lift a finger, do you?"

Kim's studio had been converted into the baby's room. By her second trimester, she'd stopped schlepping her portfolio from gallery to gallery only to be rejected. The task of selling art was exhausting. She'd begun to imagine that the people who turned her down experienced a silent glee at her disappointment. She no longer felt like proving them wrong. Now she just didn't want to give them the satisfaction of seeing her fail. And so she withdrew.

Charles was her sanctuary from all of that competition and rejection. She quit her job at the restaurant. She packed up all of her art supplies, to wait until they moved to a bigger place.

She read self-help books and meditated. She listened to relaxation recordings. She sampled essential oils and aromatherapy until Charles said the odor of eucalyptus was hurting his sinuses.

She looked for beauty in simple tasks. She tried to locate the glory of motherhood while wiping liquid green poop from her daughter's legs, stripping down the bassinet, and washing all the bedding for the third time in one day. She talked to her baby and sang to her, eliciting nothing more than a burp or the lopsided grin that indicated another poop was on the way.

Finally she found solace in a headset, with the Cranberries cranked up enough to drown the traffic noises beyond her living room window. Beyond her influence now—that's how she thought of the city, and the world. It was a spirit world made of light, and she was made of blood and vomit.

Most of all, she was bone tired. All day, while Charles was at the office, Kim fought to stay awake. It wasn't only the real fatigue that came with late night feedings and constantly paying attention to her baby's needs. She was exhausted from fighting her natural impulse to walk away from the apartment, climb aboard a #7 bus, and not come back.

She longed to stay in bed when the baby cried out, or to scream at Charles to let him know how bored she was. Drowsiness kept pulling her down toward the floor. She yearned to curl up there and forget who she was. She wanted to tumble into dreamless sleep. A few times she fell asleep standing up.

On one of these occasions she was giving the baby a bath. She stood over the plastic tub, which was carefully centered on the kitchen table. She saw her infant daughter lying in the shallow, tepid water, saw her gazing up, frowning, and then—blank.

She came to with a shock of recognition—the baby bath on top of the table, her own hands lying limp on either side of the baby's delicate chest, her daughter staring up into her eyes as if she knew. She knew.

"I'm not going to lie to you," she told the baby, who was beginning to shiver in the cooling bath. "I'm a shitty mother. You're not going to learn anything from me. But your dad's a good guy. He's going to make up for all the things I can't give you, okay?"

With that, Kim reached out to the breakfast tray she had left on the countertop all morning. She seized a fork and, without hesitation, dragged the tines across the back of her wrist. Not enough to bleed much. Not nearly enough for stitches, just enough to leave a mark.

She explained the bandage to Charles as an accident. She had let the baby's nails grow too long and had gotten scratched. It was nothing to worry about. It would heal quickly.

"You're doing a great job," Charles said. The man she loved more than anything in the world was glowing with pride. He put his arms around her. He kissed her neck and held her close.

"You see?" he said. "You're a natural."

BRIAR

THE SHELTER was nothing like the clinical institution Briar had imagined and feared, and nothing like the unpainted cement block building where her paperwork was processed while she sat in a plastic chair that was bolted to the floor of the lobby. Instead, she found herself waiting with the social worker on the doorstep of a well-built residence on a street where most of the other homes were deserted and derelict. If someone had asked her to draw a picture of a perfect country home, this might have been it, with a generous frame, bay windows, trellises, and two chimneys.

Behind the house, a meadow spread across two vacant lots. Here the air carried less of the cottonwood Briar had seen on the ride from the police station. Wildflowers bobbed above the overgrown grass in the late morning light, enticing bees, butterflies, and hummingbirds. A boy and girl who appeared to be slightly younger than Briar were striding among the grass and weeds, waving sticks and shouting. At first Briar thought they were talking to one another, but as she continued to watch, she noticed they were waving—and shouting or chanting—in her direction.

The doorbell chimed to a tune that sounded familiar, but she couldn't quite recognize it. The woman who answered was a lot like the social worker—female, early thirties, swaddled in a fluffy sweater over threadbare corduroy slacks and scuffed clogs. The kind of person Evelyn used to call a 'granola muncher.'

"Hello," said the woman whose nametag read 'Maisie.' "Welcome. You must be Briar. Come on inside."

The foyer opened into a wide hallway with double doors, leading to a living room with a fireplace, exposed rafters, and built-in cedar benches and shelves. Colorful patchwork quilts decorated the walls. Each seating area was flanked by large hand-woven baskets full of dried leaves and potpourri. A watercolor of bright yellow sunflowers and honeybees hung above the fireplace.

"This is nice," said Briar. "But I have a place to stay."

The social worker and Maisie exchanged a sympathetic look. "That's great," Maisie said. "For right now, Briar, let's get you settled. You've been through a lot. We need to fill out some paperwork. Then I'll show you to your room and we'll see about getting you a change of clothes. How does that sound?"

Briar looked down at the immaculate gray sweatpants that bunched around her waist and ankles, the blue T-shirt with a Clark County Police Department logo on one shoulder, and black ballet slippers. It was the worst outfit she'd ever worn. For the first time a wave of regret rose up in her heart. She didn't miss Ray at all. She didn't even miss her mother as much as she had expected to. But she was truly heartbroken about losing her favorite boots.

She felt no remorse for what she'd done to Tyler. He was such a loser, no one had even reported him missing. She imagined a scene of perfect indifference: Clark Middle School assuming he was skipping classes again and sending unread emails to his mother, who was probably out of town and assumed he was just sulking at home. Where was the panic? Where were the police? And what about the Amber Alert? If anybody cared about Tyler, someone would investigate eventually. By then Briar would be a member of the Davis family, and they would swear she was a good person like Tasha, beyond suspicion. All of the Davises were good people. When she joined their family, she would be good too.

"It's a waste of money for you to take care of me," she explained. "I can borrow some clothes from Tasha when I get to her house."

As she said this, she noticed how the doors had locks on both sides but no handles on the interior. Everything about the house, from the yellow paint with ruby trim to the fuzzy wall hangings, was designed to imitate a cozy bed and breakfast, probably to disguise the fact that people weren't allowed to leave. Just knowing this made Briar want to bolt, but she knew she wouldn't get far. It was smart to go along until her chances were better. She was good at this, waiting for the right moment.

Maisie introduced her to two more women. One of them, a counselor, was tall and gangly, with big gums that showed when she smiled. The other was some sort of manager. Their names were so bland Briar couldn't remember them, and had to keep referring to the tags pinned to their blouses.

Once everyone had a chance to squeeze Briar's shoulder and hold her hand and tell her things would be okay, they could all see she wasn't going to break down in front of them. The social worker gave Briar a business card with her phone number and said goodbye.

The gangly counselor spent an hour with her in the 'day room,' a bright hall with a vaulted ceiling and a locked window. Their conversation was confidential, the woman assured her. There was nothing to worry about. It was only an assessment, a check-in requirement to see 'where she was at' and 'what she needed.'

During their chat, Briar kept glancing out the window. She could see the green and fragrant meadow from here, with its assortment of wildflowers. She noticed the boy and girl playing there advanced a bit closer to the house and then retreated, advanced and retreated. Every time she looked away and then checked again, they were in a different spot. It was irritating to her, comparing their freedom outdoors to her situation. She wondered why they weren't in school, and imagined their mother must be their teacher, as hers had been.

"...And it's perfectly natural to have conflicted feelings about what happened." The counselor was droning on. Briar realized she'd stopped listening for a while.

"Conflicted?"

"Two different feelings at the same time," said the counselor with a gummy smile.

"Oh," said Briar. "All I know is what I told the cops."

"Right," said the counselor. "I'm sure you were very helpful. What I'd like to ask you now is to feel free to talk about anything. Not only about what happened. Any feelings or memories or worries you might have. Whatever comes to mind, it's all right to talk about it. Every person here is ready and willing to help, any time."

Briar considered this. She knew the woman was lying. She was exactly the kind of 'helping person' Briar's mom had always warned her about. From the earliest age she could remember—maybe three or four—she was told to avoid anyone with a kind expression who offered to help her. These people were the worst kind of liar, Evelyn explained, feeding on the tragedies of others and pretending to make the world a better place.

"Is my mom going to prison?" she asked the counselor.

"Oh," said the woman, clearly surprised by the nature of the question. She leafed through her notes, located the information she was after. "Evelyn Kenny..."

"Gamel," said Briar. "Our name is Gamel."

The woman leafed through her notes again. "According to your school records, your mother registered you as Briar Kenny."

"I know," said Briar. "But our name is Gamel. Ray's name was Kenny, and he's dead."

"Yes," the counselor said solemnly. "Your mother is receiving the best care available. Her condition will be carefully evaluated..."

"She's crazy," said Briar.

"Generally speaking, I like to stick to more clinical terms when describing..." the counselor began.

"She told the cops she killed her husband," said Briar.

"I see."

"She didn't have to do that. Everybody would think it was an accident. But she started screaming how she killed her husband. Except Ray was just her boyfriend," Briar explained. "What's wrong with her?" She genuinely wanted to know what would make Evelyn behave the way she did. It was weird, and it bothered Briar that no one had an explanation.

"Naturally you feel concern for your mother," the counselor said. "Would you like to speak with her?"

"No," said Briar.

"Maybe at a later date." The counselor raised her eyebrows, urging the right answer, but Briar couldn't say it.

"No," she said.

"Of course you don't have to," the counselor said and folded her large hands clumsily in her lap.

Briar studied the woman's face, the fine wrinkles creeping outward from the corners of her eyes and mouth. Her lipstick was crimson, and she wore her brown hair in a loose French bun-style Briar had seen in a fashion magazine her mother liked. It struck Briar as odd, these vanities, on a woman working at a shelter.

"Can I call my friend Tasha?" she asked. "I'm supposed to be at school. Can the Davises pick me up later?"

The woman's long, kind expression mirrored that of the social worker, and the police officers, and Maisie. Briar expected most of the people she met from now on would look down their noses at her in that horsey way, once they heard her story. They would feel sorry for the girl with the burned-up home and a crazy mother claiming she murdered her husband.

She wondered what that was all about. She could only guess Evelyn had finally lost it. Maybe she'd held it together as long as she could, when Briar was a kid. Over the years sometimes she'd gone nuts, but she held down a job and paid rent and bought groceries. She had been a mother first, a little bit crazy but reliable. Then Ray had gotten his hooks into her. He told Evelyn what she wanted to hear. Every word of it was a lie. Ray had broken what was left of her.

"Well," said the counselor, "tell you what. I'll make a few calls. We'll see what we can do. Meanwhile, I'll have one of the aides contact your school and send your homework assignments by email, how's that? Then you won't miss any lessons."

* * *

Briar couldn't care less about homework or falling behind. Going to school was a fairly new experience. She often forgot to collect her textbooks from her locker, or left them because she didn't want to carry a backpack. She didn't see how the grades she earned could change any part of her life. She was content to glide through with a C average.

This life in Skillute, the trailer park, Clark Middle School, it all seemed like one more temporary stop until she met Tasha. Now she had to convince the counselor and the social worker to let her live with the Davis family. Then things would work out. It would all be worth it once she joined the Davis household for good.

She was surprised to find how little she missed Evelyn. Almost as surprised as she was when her mother confessed to killing Ray.

Briar had expected both of them to die in the fire. All of her fantasies revolved around being an orphan, throwing herself on the mercy of the Davis family, and becoming one of them. She never considered what would happen if Evelyn woke up and stumbled outdoors during the fire. The dazed expression on Evelyn's face, half asleep and half drunk, served as a reminder of how much was beyond Briar's control.

She'd been quick enough to respond, to act as if they were both lucky survivors. She was planning to tell the cops how glad she was to see her mother come walking out of the fire. But then Evelyn saw Ray's corpse and started spewing her crazy confession. That was when Briar decided less was more. She didn't know anything. Ray was cleaning a guitar. Everyone went to bed. She woke up gagging from the smoke and ran outside. That was enough.

She wondered if it was wrong not to feel sad. What she'd done had killed Ray and put her mother in an asylum, but Evelyn had slipped away from her long ago. If Briar were honest, there was only a fading outline of the hurt she used to feel, a wound inflicted and never completely healed, but often forgotten in favor of interesting distractions.

Evelyn had had plenty of opportunities to make things right. Briar had given her every chance almost every day since she'd met Rayburn Kenny to come to her senses, to stop wearing tight dresses that made her look tacky and old, to sober up and act like a mom again. But it never happened.

When Briar considered things in this way, it all made sense. She had been more than fair.

She thought about the fire itself, and its power to change everything. The part she loved was hearing the *snap* of wood as the guitars caught the flames, one by one, and split open. There was a distinct *zing* as the strings popped loose, and it was almost music.

ORTON & GRETCHEN

THE MEADOW was buzzing. Bees and hummingbirds flitted from leaf to petal, dabbling, searching, and moving on.

Orton crouched in the grass and filled his hands with dirt. He rubbed the palms together. He'd been doing this, off and on, for years. Nothing took the bloodstains away.

Gretchen tiptoed, pretending to be a ballerina. When she spotted orange hawkweed or yellow archangel she would reach down, yank it out of the soil, and toss it on the pile she was collecting. After the flowers dried and the leaves went brown, they would be perfect for her bouquet.

"The girl doesn't look very upset," said Gretchen with a nod toward the shelter.

"I bet she thinks all the bad things are over now and she's home free," said Orton.

"Isn't she?" Gretchen asked.

"Nah. She's got no idea."

"Other people have stayed in the shelter," said Gretchen.

"But they didn't kill anybody," said Orton. "They're not bad ones. When something evil gets inside a person and that person doesn't have a bad streak, it gets confused—like a hornet in a box. This girl's just right."

Gretchen considered this. "Are you scared?" she asked.

Orton crouched and picked up another handful of dirt. He considered the shelter. From here he could see Briar looking out the window.

"Well," he said, "I'm not stupid."

"You want to say the prayer again, to ward off witches?" she asked.

"Nah," he said. "She's no witch."

"You want to say it again?" she asked, her lips pursed in a mournful expression.

"Yeah," he told her. "Say the prayer."

TASHA

SHE COULDN'T think of anything else to do. She felt itchy and restless. Her only friend was imprisoned in some state or county shelter and Tasha had no control over anything, least of all her parents.

They didn't seem to understand what Briar was going through. They agreed that she could come to stay until the end of the term, in early June, but they weren't doing much about it. Once they called the authorities and offered temporary care, they just sat back and waited for things to happen and for people to call them. It was driving Tasha crazy. She was afraid for Briar, but also afraid that Briar might talk about Tyler and how they left him unconscious—not right away, or because she wanted to. It would happen against her will.

Tasha decided to Google the shelter. If she wasn't allowed to visit until a determination was made, she could at least do a little research on the place. She had plenty of time. She had taken to bed in her winter pajamas since the night Briar was taken into custody, and she had no intention of going to school again until her friend was set free.

It was a shaky revolution, and Tasha was frankly surprised by its effectiveness. Neither of her parents insisted. Both assured her that Briar would be okay and would join them as soon as her social worker gave the okay. So she curled up in bed and read the brief history of Hope Haven on her laptop.

* * *

The shelter was originally the home of a prosperous Skillute couple, Henry and Alicia Colquitt. The property consisted of a large brick house on three acres of land, with a doublewide trailer that served as Henry's church. The trailer had been removed and sold when the church failed.

Known as a charitable man, the preacher had attempted to open a center much like Hope Haven on another property owned by his family. The vacant lot had since been auctioned off to pay Henry Colquitt's legal fees.

The reluctance of his neighbors to permit construction of a shelter on the land might have been related to a series of scandals several years prior. Colquitt's mother was a suspicious character who had died in a fire under mysterious circumstances. The woman had a reputation as a sort of healer. There were rumors of unlicensed midwifery and sketchy medicinal practices, all leading the less educated of her acquaintances to speculate that she was part of a coven of witches. Not that anyone believed in witches; they just thought the woman was crazy.

Local authorities took none of these rumors seriously. They were at a loss to explain Henry Colquitt's subsequent actions. Regarded as a gentle and good-natured man, he had apparently become depressed over the lack of support for his plans.

Henry suffered a psychotic break while snowed in with his wife during a blizzard in the winter of 2014. The subsequent murder of Alicia and an attack on a young girl, whose name was withheld from news media, led to his arrest and conviction.

Although the records were sealed, it was rumored that Henry believed he could resurrect the dead. When police were called to his home by the parents of the murdered child, Henry shouted for them to leave him be while he did God's work.

At the time the Wikipedia entry was last edited, Colquitt was serving a life sentence in the state penitentiary with no possibility of parole.

KIM

ALL OF the infant care manuals and all of Kim's friends had warned her. Even her mother lectured her long distance.

"Breastfeed for nine months, ten if you feel good about it. Plenty of people say longer, but I don't think it's necessary. Besides, babies develop a lot faster than they did when I had you. They start teething sooner these days, and you don't want to put yourself through that while you're breastfeeding."

"Thanks, mom. I'm okay," Kim said. "Are you coming to visit the baby?"

"I wish I could, dear," her mother said, as always. "It's our busy season. I don't think the office can get along without me. You know how stupid my assistant is."

Despite the advice, Kim weaned the baby early, at three months, and went on a high-protein diet. Her studio was gone, sacrificed to make room for the bassinet and playpen and crib. She slept so little she was beginning to dream while awake. Every inch of her home and her flesh had been given over to the baby for what seemed like eons. She thought that if she couldn't recover what was left of the body she once knew, she would go out of her mind. Her weight appeared to be the only area where she had any control whatsoever, and she was staking her claim to it.

She knew she had a small trust fund waiting, but she felt ashamed of her lack of income. She'd been turned down by all of the companies where she applied for work after the baby came. She never even made it to the interview phase. One hiring manager asked her—in a manner so obviously delicate she found it insulting—if she was ready to return to the workforce. Another gave her a mini-lecture on the importance of balancing family and professional life, and expressed concern for her abandoned baby. One guy had the audacity to say he just didn't trust the fluctuating commitments of a woman in the middle of drastic hormonal changes.

Kim wished she could sue somebody. She wanted to complain. She wanted to step into a time machine and become the person she'd been a year earlier. She wanted her slight hips and flat chest, her careless way of sauntering down the sidewalk, and the cute clothes that went with her original body, her true self.

She set a new schedule, even more grueling than before. No matter how tired she was from late nights with the baby, three days a week she was up at dawn, before Charles left for the office, doing double rounds on the treadmill and rowing machine at her local gym. When the extra inches failed to dissolve, she cried. When her period failed to appear on time, she ignored it and worked out harder.

Then one morning, waiting for the pedestrian light at the corner of Broadway and Pine, sipping a macchiato, she had a terrifying thought. Fighting an urge to walk in front of a bus, she headed to the pharmacy.

Later that day, after confirming her worst fear—she was, indeed, pregnant again—Kim didn't discuss the matter with Charles, who was still besotted with their infant daughter. She made an appointment, arranged for a friend to babysit that afternoon, and paid the clinic in cash.

She explained her need to stay in bed for a couple days by saying she was rundown from all of the exercise. Charles took time off from work to mind the baby. He brought her cups of miso and reminded her, again and again, that it was okay to slow down and take care of her own needs. The baby was important, but not more important than Kim and her happiness. When his words made her cry, he apologized.

MRS. TED
VAN DEVERE

SHE RAISED a glass of Argentine Malbec to her lips. The first sip was silk. Then it tingled, leaving the flavors of black cherry liqueur, black raspberry, and tobacco on her tongue.

Through the sheer curtains in her living room, she could see the burnt-out shell of the Kenny family's mobile home next door. It reminded Mrs. Ted Van Devere of a wooly mammoth skeleton she had seen at a natural history museum as a child. In the light of dawn it had resembled the wreck of the *Peter Iredale* on the Oregon shore, all of its inner secrets sheared open and left to the elements. The steel frame stood intact, but the walls had burned away, so that one could look right through from one side to the other. The outer walls, made of wood, survived only at the far corners of the structure, and created the illusion of bracing what remained. The front door was visible, but its metal screen had warped and twisted with heat. All of the family's belongings were spread across the floor and on the ground in front of the trailer. At least a dozen guitar necks lay among the ruins. No longer smoldering, each object seemed a blackened silhouette of its former self.

She had replayed in memory every word of her conversation with the Kenny girl. No matter how she interpreted what they'd said, Mrs. Van Devere couldn't find a reason for what had happened. Despite this, she blamed herself for failing to recognize the girl's state of mind. They had spoken only a few hours before the catastrophe, and her young neighbor had revealed nothing of her intentions.

Or, she wondered, could she be entirely wrong? Was it possible that Mrs. Kenny, that distraught, confused woman, was telling the truth and was responsible for the fire? It didn't make sense, but it was the version of events accepted by the police and the local paper.

Everyone responding to the incident had moved on. The explanation offered to them was satisfying, and they had gone on to other emergencies. Mrs. Kenny was interviewed and taken to a hospital. Her daughter was in the care of the county. Only Rayburn Kenny wasn't able to move on, his pathetically charred body hauled out on a stretcher, bits of his skin flaking off to be carried by the breeze. Even now there were probably fragments of the man mingled with cottonwood, sailing past Mrs. Van Devere's window.

She longed to sleep, although it was too early. She wanted to leave this place and soar above the trailer park and into the sky, but she knew she couldn't set aside her suspicion. She had a responsibility to see the girl and speak with her. In her present state the girl would be a perfect target.

These people passing through, they had no idea of the dangers buried here. Even if they'd known the history of the town, and none of them seemed to, they wouldn't be safe. The thought of parents dragging their children here to keep them away from all the awful influences of city life, it made Mrs. Van Devere want to scream. Nevertheless, she sipped her Malbec and waited. She needed to prepare a viable excuse for meeting with the Kenny girl, and adopt the innocuous appearance she employed for these day-to-day encounters with people.

BRIAR

THE COUNSELOR droned on for what seemed like days. Then she touched Briar on the shoulder and assured her that everything would work out, no matter how bleak it might appear at the moment.

As soon as the counselor turned away, Maisie took her place. They were like a relay team. Every time one staff member left, another stepped in to repeat the litany of advice and reassurances, so that Briar was never alone until evening.

"You're going to love your room," said G.G., a ponytailed woman who'd just spent two minutes explaining the funny origins of her nickname—information Briar tuned out.

"And my Bible," Briar said under her breath.

"Sorry?" said G.G.

"Nothing," said Briar. "Where do I sleep?"

G.G. led her upstairs to a bedroom in the back corner of the house. The first thing Briar noticed was the lack of doors. From the desk parked at the top of the stairs, all the way down the hall, every chamber they passed was open, yet she couldn't see a thing in the rooms. Without doors, they resembled a row of open mouths. Briar imagined a busy, mad dentist lining up patients in chairs on wheels. It was the first thought she'd had all day that didn't include Tasha, or escape, or the fire.

"You like to keep an eye on the inmates, huh?" Briar half-joked.

"We don't use the term 'inmate.' Think of yourself as a guest," said G.G. "An honored and welcome guest. The doors were a trade-off when Hope Haven was first developed. You see, every room has a window. If there were doors they would have to be locked, and the windows would have to be blocked off, as a safety precaution. We feel this is a better option. You have a view of your own, isn't that nice?"

"Yes. Nice," said Briar. She noticed the window in her room had no handle, and the edges were sealed. There was no way to escape. The false good cheer of the place was choking her, making her feel trapped, swaddled in charity.

G.G. opened a drawer in the bedroom and pointed out the T-shirts and jeans in Briar's size. She had such an expression of smug satisfaction, Briar felt compelled to reward her by saying, "Very nice. Thank you."

As they surveyed the cozy space, Briar wondered why G.G. wasn't bothering to whisper or dim the table lamp, despite the obvious presence of another girl asleep in one of the twin beds. She also found it odd that she was sharing a room when there appeared to be plenty of vacancies upstairs. But she was tired of hearing about the policies and pleasantries of Hope Haven, so she didn't ask any more questions.

"The bathroom is next door," said G.G. "And if you need anything at all, I'll be right down there." She pointed to the desk at the top of the stairs.

Briar managed a grin and a nod. As soon as G.G. walked away, she turned off the lamp. The only illumination was an amber glow from a sconce above the desk in the hall, combined with the soft white beams of moonlight through her window.

She lay down on the empty bed. It was wonderful, with a firm mattress and fresh, clean sheets smelling of lilac. She understood how the girl in the other bed had slept through her conversation with G.G. Briar could barely keep her eyes open. This was exactly how she'd felt at Tasha's house, lying in a comfortable bed for the first time in years.

This was what she'd resented most of all about the long haul with Ray from one miserable town to another. Everywhere they'd stayed, conditions were a little worse than before. She had vacated her room in Tacoma and its privacy for a porch hammock, followed by an air mattress on the floor. The trailer was the last straw, with its crummy sofa bed with squeaky springs, located in the middle of the living room where it collected beer stains and crumbs. She had never felt more adrift and lonely than on the nights she spent there, staring at the ceiling and praying for lightning to strike Ray dead. When she thought of him now, it was with a wicked grin.

She listened for the sound of her roommate breathing or snoring. There was nothing, nothing at all to hold her back from the deep, luxurious darkness of sleep.

* * *

Briar sat up and blinked in the pool of moonlight spilling across her bed. Her roommate was gone, the blanket tossed back in haste. As her eyes adjusted, Briar saw her own shadow cast on the window.

She was sure the silhouette belonged to her, until it moved when she did not. Whatever it was, in the shape of a girl, heavy-set or swaddled in layers of clothes, raised its hands and held them like blinders while it peered in.

Briar tried to stay frozen, waiting for the girl, or the wide shadow of a girl, to make a sound. Minutes passed. Against her will, at last, her body sank heavily back into the sheets. Next time she was aware of watching the window, the frame was empty.

* * *

During the day she kept up with her homework. She toured the shelter again, ate lunch, asked Maisie the name of her roommate.

"Sorry?" Maisie said.

"The girl who was asleep when I went to bed," Briar said.

"I guess you were really exhausted," said Maisie. "You and Miranda are the only guests at the moment. Miranda is staying in the downstairs bedroom."

Briar considered pursuing the subject but thought better of it. The last thing she needed was the counselor reporting she was as crazy as her mom. Medication would follow, and doubled counseling sessions, and she would never get out of this place. She played along with Maisie and let her think what Briar had seen in her room was a trick of shadow and light. Maybe it was.

On the second night she stayed awake as long as possible. When staff members stopped by, she pretended to be asleep. This occurred three times and finally, in fact, she slipped under.

* * *

"Let me be," she said. "Leave me alone."

"Come on," said the girl. "Get up!"

Briar's arms were being pulled, and she followed. The window was open, the glass broken out of the frame. She stepped forward and laughed. The house had so many security and safety rules and yet here they were, two girls alone, climbing onto the roof. Her feet edged along the rough, cold tiles until she reached a chimney.

"Why didn't I think of the fireplace?" she said.

"You don't want to crawl through a nasty, filthy chimney," said the girl, who wore a heavy coat and scarf. "All you have to do is look at a window and take a step."

Briar held her arms out at her sides and turned in a slow circle. From the rooftop she could see Skillute spilling in all directions

126

around her. She stood at the exact center.

Down a twisted path and through the woods three girls ran, shouting and laughing, trailing thin fingers of smoke. On the lawn at Tasha's house a family camped out in tents and plywood shacks, cooking a wild hare over a crackling fire. Trucks loaded with lumber barreled over dirt roads. A woman wearing deerskin hung strips of cedar on a rack to dry. In the garden where Tasha and Briar liked to meet, the windmills were spinning with bright colors, and birds darted from the cottage windows to the feeders and back. Directly below the roof, on the ground, she saw a man on his knees praying, with the bodies of a woman and a young girl—the girl in the heavy coat and scarf—stretched out beside him. In the night air a million tiny, white clouds of cottonwood swirled.

"Hear them singing?" the girl whispered.

Briar cupped a hand to her ear and heard a shrill chorus overhead. "Is it coming from the cottonwood?" she asked.

The girl held up both her hands and Briar could see she was wearing gloves. The lower half of her coat was crimson with gore. She smiled, baring a set of bloodstained teeth. "Witches," she said. "Witches."

* * *

The next morning the sky was overcast. Briar woke with the dull sensations of having slept badly. She needed a minute to remember where she was, and why. Beyond the doorframe two women were whispering, and she wondered if she might still be dreaming.

"She hasn't cried or asked to see her mother."

"She's still in shock. It will come."

"Should we call Dr. Langley? In case there's something we've overlooked?"

"Not necessary. No. Let her take her own time. She has a visitor scheduled for this morning, doesn't she?"

The voices faded. The women were moving away.

Briar stretched and noticed she was now wearing only a T-shirt and underwear. Her sweatpants lay puddled on the floor near the window. The twin bed next to her was empty and neatly made up.

Beside myself, she thought. The words rattled against one another in her head. She tried saying them out loud.

"Beside myself."

The voice was achingly familiar, but it wasn't hers. She tried to recall the voice of the girl in the heavy coat, who lured her in her dream. Nothing came to mind.

"Briar," she said, and the sound of it was strangely foreign. She knew her name wasn't Briar anymore, but she decided to keep it until she could find a way out of this place.

* * *

Breakfast was served in the large dining hall downstairs. Upon entering, Briar was surprised to see Mrs. Dead Lavender—it was an odd name and she didn't know what it meant—seated at the end of a long table. Urged by Maisie, the girl calling herself Briar accepted a chair to the left of the old woman.

"I'll be right outside if you need anything," said Maisie before she left them alone together, for there were no other diners.

Briar stared at the trays full of muffins and fruit. She wondered why there was so much food. She watched condensation forming on a glass of orange juice and waited for the old woman to begin the conversation.

"Your tattoo," said Mrs. Dead Lavender.

"What about it?" Briar followed the woman's gaze and touched herself on the neck.

"It's changed colors," the old woman told her. "The leaves have changed to green."

"Maybe you just don't remember me very well," said Briar. She was searching for a distinct memory of the woman before her, and finding only flashes of light and the aroma of something sickly sweet.

"Have you spoken with anyone?" Mrs. Dead Lavender asked.

"That's all I've been doing since I got here," said Briar. "All they do here is talk and talk and talk."

The woman studied Briar silently. "Tell me something," she said at last. "What do you see on this wall?" She pointed to a spot directly opposite where they were seated.

Briar turned her attention to the wall and saw pale yellow paint, nothing more. But if she concentrated on that one section, she could almost *taste* something, a bad flavor like rotten meat. Once she thought of it, she couldn't get it out of her mind.

"Nothing," she said.

"No shape beneath the paint?" Mrs. Dead Lavender asked. "No movement?"

Briar turned sharply. "Is this a test?" she asked. "Are you testing me?"

"In a manner of speaking," the woman said.

"Why?"

"Don't you know?" asked Mrs. Dead Lavender, a stranger, a silver-haired lady in a linen suit with a violet scarf loosely tied around her neck, all forming a kaleidoscopic image that shifted and settled, shifted and settled into place.

"No," said Briar. "How would I know?" She snatched a blueberry muffin from a tray and picked it into pieces but didn't eat. She wasn't hungry. She had been ravenous the night before, and exhausted, but now she felt—wired, buzzing with a sort of electric current.

"Have you met any other children here?" Mrs. Dead Lavender asked. Her voice was steady, unnaturally so, as though she were measuring not only the words but also the shape and sound of each one.

"No," said Briar. "Why are you talking that way?"

"In what way?"

Briar flinched and made a strange sound—a swift, involuntary intake of air through a corner of her mouth. She was surprised by the suddenness of it. She had heard Evelyn describe how her grandmother, now long gone, used to suffer little spasms, nervous tics that caused her head to bobble. Briar wondered for the first time if this could be an inherited illness. She wasn't accustomed to her body doing uncontrollable things. She would have to practice staying steady.

"What do you see on the wall?" the woman asked again.

This time, when Briar turned her attention to the yellow paint, something new occurred. The more she concentrated, the more she thought she could see the outline of a face, not human but animal-like, maybe a mask, trying to emerge from the wall. Its nostrils protruded and retracted with a snort.

"What do you see?" Mrs. Dead Lavender asked.

"Nothing!" Briar snapped. She pinched off a bit of muffin and crammed it into her mouth. It tasted like salt. She knew the woman was interrogating her, studying her, not only her expression, but something else, something more. "It's good," she said.

"Are you sure?" the woman asked.

"Who are you?"

"Just a visitor," the woman said.

"Me, too," said Briar. "I'm just visiting this place."

"No," said Mrs. Dead Lavender. "I think you've been here for a long, long time."

Briar stopped chewing, and her mouth hung open. When she realized what she was doing, she closed her mouth and swallowed. The bread tasted like dirt. She heard a snort and turned to the spot on the far wall where an elk's head hung, both alive and dead, working its jaw as if it could break free and run away.

"Listen carefully," said the woman. "If you're playing with me, Briar, this is a dangerous game. You have no idea how dangerous. There is a malicious spirit at work."

It was Briar's turn to snort—a short, sharp laugh. "You made a pun," she said. "Ha ha ha," she intoned without a hint of mirth. "Dangerous *game*. Ha ha ha."

"Do you understand why you're here?" the old woman asked.

This elicited a sideways stare from Briar. She knew what she was doing, but she didn't feel she could stop. Everything was beginning to seem natural to her, as if she were speaking and moving and living for the first time in her own skin.

"Evelyn killed her husband," she said.

"No," said Mrs. Dead Lavender. "Your mother is in a hospital. She's confused, and medicated. She doesn't remember what happened. But she will. One day she'll figure it out. Do you understand? She'll admit what really happened. She'll tell everyone what her daughter did, capriciously and naively."

Briar sat up, straight-backed in her chair. She looked at the old woman and recognized her.

"You said people survive awful things."

"Yes," said the woman. "I wanted to comfort you. Not to urge you on."

"You don't know as much as you pretend, do you?" said Briar. Her voice echoed in the room, an adult voice, weighted and sure. "You don't know Evelyn and you don't know *me*."

"Briar," said the woman. "Your name is Briar, a part of you. And if you can still understand me, I think these things are happening because of what you did."

"I haven't done anything," said Briar. "I'm a child." She picked up another piece of muffin and popped it in her mouth. It tasted like rancid butter.

"Most children won't work. Infants won't work for long. They're only a temporary shelter. They don't serve the purpose. Only a living person who's committed a crime will do," said Mrs. Dead Lavender. She leaned closer and studied Briar, gazing deeply into her eyes. "*You've* figured this out, haven't you?"

"Blah blah blah," said Briar.

"Listen to me, Briar, if you can hear me," said the woman. "You killed someone. You set fire to a man and you watched him burn to death. Now this thing, living in this place and waiting, knows you. It knows where you live and it knows how to live inside you."

Briar smiled. "Then why did Evelyn take the blame?"

Mrs. Dead Lavender hesitated. "I don't know," she admitted.

"Ha!" said Briar. "Ha ha ha." She stood up and called out, "Maisie!"

When Maisie opened the door, Briar strode out of the dining room and said, "Our visit is over." To the old woman she shouted, "Thanks for stopping by!"

* * *

For the rest of the week, Briar spent most of her time in her room. She was allowed to take short walks outdoors if accompanied by staff. She didn't like to go outside, because she kept spotting the boy and girl from the meadow. Sometimes they followed her. Sometimes they were hiding in the trees. No one else could see them, and this was troubling. She avoided the dining room, because the walls were now lined with animal heads that kept chewing and snorting at her.

As long she followed a strict routine, she wasn't aware of the buzzing in her head. It only grew louder if she began to mull over the conversation with Mrs. Dead Lavender, whom Maisie called Mrs. Ted Van Devere. She wondered if the old woman had spoken with anyone else, but she doubted they'd believe her crazy rambling.

Briar tried to smile, but only when people expected it. She completed her homework on time and went to bed early. She ate meals from a TV tray in the living room along with the shelter's other guest, the woman named Miranda. This was a trial in itself, since the woman never stopped talking.

"My husband and I had a nice home," said Miranda. "My husband was a good man. He worked hard. My kids were beautiful..." She told the same story every day.

Miranda seemed like a name for a young woman and she was older, maybe forty. Her hair was fastened back in a fancy clip. She wore loose, flowing, bright-colored housedresses with sandals, and she had a silver ring on one of her toes.

132

Miranda told Briar she had lost her home. Two years ago her husband died and left her broke. She couldn't pay her taxes. The state took her children and gave them to foster homes. She had stayed with a friend for a while, but when her friend moved away, she had nowhere to live. She slept outside for a few nights. First she slept in a garden attached to a shopping mall, but the property owners hired security guards to walk around at night, waking people up and making them move on.

She found another spot, hidden inside a crate behind an arts and crafts shop. She thought it would be safer there than sleeping under the freeway overpass, where most of the homeless people camped. She said she had never been on her own, not like that, and she was afraid.

On her third night sleeping behind the crafts shop, she woke up during the night. Outside the crate she heard scratching. Next she heard an animal sniffing its way from one end of the crate to the other and back. She tried to block the hole she used as an entrance, but she was hungry and weak.

When the animal—a dog, she didn't recognize the breed—spotted Miranda, it bit her on the arm. The owner called out the dog's name and pulled it away, but Miranda's arm was really bleeding, so the dog owner called an ambulance.

She had to have a bunch of shots, and the hospital kept her for a week. When she was released, she still didn't have anywhere to go. That's how she ended up at Hope Haven. On her arm she bore the jagged scars, shaped like canine teeth.

Miranda said the shelter used to be the home of a preacher. The man was good, she said, and kind. But he had a nervous breakdown and murdered his wife. When the police arrested him, he told them he shouldn't have been 'interrupted.'

They found him with a girl who was unconscious and half-buried in the snow. (This was where Briar began to really lose interest.) The cops pieced together from his testimony and what the girl's parents said that he was performing some kind of ritual. ("Blah

blah blah," Briar whispered.) He said this was his destiny. The girl didn't wake up. She was in a coma to this day. ("Oh, that's terrible," said Briar. "So sad.") Her parents didn't even know how she got to the preacher's house, so the police decided she must have been abducted. (And on and on she went, while Briar's eyes closed and opened, closed and opened.)

Miranda's story never varied. No matter how many times she told it, she began, "My husband and I had a nice home. My husband was a good man…"

Only once did Miranda pause in the middle of this tale. She reached a hand toward Briar's neck, as if she meant to touch her tattoo. But instead she grew agitated, and had to be sedated and put to bed.

THE DAVIS FAMILY

THE SIGHT of Briar with her charity duffel bag slung over one shoulder prompted tears, but not from Kim and Charles. Tasha pushed past her parents and strode down the driveway as though she hadn't seen her friend in years. She threw her arms around Briar, pulled the duffel bag from her shoulder, and led her indoors.

The Davises had agreed to all conditions and accepted the terms of the foster care contract. The county provided a small stipend and Medicaid for any of the girl's health care needs. She was required to meet with a social worker twice a month and attend counseling sessions twice a week, but none of this was scheduled yet. Everyone understood that Briar was going through a period of adjustment.

All that night, the girls chattered away in Tasha's room. Kim and Charles let them be. He reasoned a good heart-to-heart might help Briar feel at home. Kim asked why he'd want her to feel at home.

"Remember, this is for Tasha," he said. They sat in the kitchen, drinking wine. They'd allowed the girls to have dinner on trays in Tasha's room, and then they cleaned up the kitchen and opened a bottle of Merlot.

"Is it?" Kim asked.

"What do you mean?" Charles asked. When she didn't answer right away, he reached out and took her hand. "Kim, we need to be patient. It's only for a little while."

"Then what?" she said. "We become the heroes? Tasha thinks we're cool?"

"Maybe," he said. "Why not?"

She sighed and withdrew her hand from his. "What if they don't become tired of one another? What if Tasha wants to visit the girl after she goes to live with her relatives?"

"First of all," he said, "her name is Briar. Objectifying her won't make this any easier. Second, it's natural that Tasha would form this—this bond with a girl her age."

Kim gave him a desperate look.

"It makes sense," he said. "The more we make of it, and the more we protest, the more she's going to pull away from us. Third, by the time the social worker locates relatives willing to take her in, Briar and Tasha will be just like any other girlfriends."

"Meaning what?"

"They won't cling so much," he said. "They'll Skype and text and lose interest in one another when they start high school. A thousand other distractions will come along. Then we'll have to cope with all of *that*."

Kim sipped her wine.

"What else is bothering you?" he asked.

She rolled her eyes. "Everything," she said. "There's just—*something*—wrong with her. Can't you see it?"

Charles glanced at the entrance to the kitchen, then down the hall. They could still hear the girls laughing and talking in Tasha's room. "She's traumatized," he said. "Why do you think she has to see the social worker and a therapist? It's a hell of a thing for a fourteen-year-old to go through, seeing her stepfather, or anyone, die like that."

"Do you think she actually saw what happened to him?"

"I don't know," he said. "Let's not be morbid."

"Under the circumstances…"

"Kim," he said. "We have a choice. Let's make this experience as normal as possible."

"Normal."

"For their sake," he said. "And ours."

* * *

Double feature night was a long-standing Davis tradition. Briar complimented Kim and Charles on everything, from the home-made gluten-free pizza with sugar-free pop to the streaming selections, *La La Land* and *Singin' in the Rain*.

They gathered in the living room, the sunken square with exposed concrete columns and wood panels. Built into the central wall was a gas fireplace. On an adjacent wall above the flat-screen TV and speakers hung a large canvas, an abstract of a scarlet cylinder revolving in space against a gray background.

"Is that one of your paintings?" Briar asked.

"No," Kim said. "This is a Sophie Britt. It was a gift from Charles. I gave up all of that a long time ago."

Something had changed about the girl's manner and bearing, but no one could put their finger on it. She was more formal, more reserved, more grownup than she had seemed before the fire. This was understandable, according to Charles, and Kim agreed. What she couldn't explain was the tattoo on Briar's neck. She could have sworn the leaves used to be brown. Now the girl kept it covered most of the time, sporting an out-of-season scarf wherever she went. Only when she let down her guard and forgot the scarf, Kim caught another glimpse of the tattoo and wondered how she could have been wrong about its details.

"Why did you quit painting?" Briar asked.

Charles excused himself to fetch more soda from the kitchen. Kim watched him go before answering the question.

"There comes a time for every so-called artist to measure what it costs to do what she does and decide if it's worth it. For me, being a mother came first."

Tasha smirked. "I thought you quit painting before I was born," she said.

"Your dad and I were planning to have a family," Kim said. "The fact is, you can't do everything. Everyone says you can, but you can't. You have to decide what you want most and commit to it."

Charles returned. He smiled and put a steadying hand on her shoulder. "We're glad you decided on us. Right, Tash?"

* * *

After everyone turned in for the night, Tasha and Briar lay awake in their beds. Tasha giggled.

"What was that all about?" she asked.

"Sorry?"

"Asking my mom about her paintings," Tasha said. "Were you being polite? You don't have to be."

"No," said Briar. "I'm really interested. Why did she quit?"

"I don't know," said Tasha. "The same reason most people give up on art, or music, or whatever. I guess she wasn't good enough."

"Have you seen any of her work?"

"No," said Tasha. "She never showed me her portfolio or anything, if that's what you mean. She said it was all junk and she didn't have her own style or anything."

"So she decided to have a family instead?" Briar asked.

"Yeah," said Tasha. "I guess."

"How sad. What a terrible waste."

"Thanks a lot!" Tasha laughed.

"Well," said Briar. "If I loved to do one thing, I don't think I would give it up for anything or anybody."

"So?"

"Doesn't it make you wonder?" said Briar. "What happened?

Why did she work at it for such a long time and then just stop—boom—never touched it again?"

"I don't know," said Tasha.

"Maybe," said Briar. "Maybe she needs to believe she wasn't good enough as an artist. Otherwise her sacrifice would be awful. She'd just be another stay-at-home mom with a part-time job."

"Sorry?"

"She's sort of a martyr," Briar said. Her expression loosened a bit, and she said more lightly, "Like my mom. Don't you think?"

Tasha considered this for a while. "Do you think you'll ever go and visit her?" she asked.

"Why?" Briar shook her head. "They can't make me visit her, can they?"

"No," said Tasha. "I don't think so. But it's normal to want to see her. I mean, it's okay if you want to."

"Of course," said Briar. She thought it over. "Yes, you're right. It's normal."

They fell silent, Tasha contemplating all of the things she didn't know about her friend, and Briar listening to the whir of thoughts in her own head.

* * *

That night Kim dreamed of smoke, the distant lowing of animals in distress, patterns of dense white and gray moving across the air, shifting like sheets on a clothesline. She slept fitfully. In the brief intervals when she lay awake, staring at the green light of her alarm clock, she was filled with dread. She blamed herself for indulging in a couple of glasses of wine before bed.

At dawn she pulled on her robe and eased quietly downstairs. She drank a cup of coffee and considered what Briar had said the night before. The girl's words had acted as a strange sort of balm. Talking about her painting after so many years made Kim wonder what she would create now, if she had stuck with it.

A mere question posed by a teenager gave her a warm glow, a longing she hadn't felt in years. It was both exquisite and embarrassing. She didn't want to admit that all the things she had—a husband she loved, a wonderful daughter, a beautiful home—might not be enough after all.

While she pondered, she noticed the sky. Examined through the glass doors of the deck, the air was somehow thick and gauzelike. She gazed past the lawn, over the slender patch of woods between her home and the road, to an abandoned field where the ruins of an old barn stood precariously. The gray sky vaulted over the landscape, clotted with cottonwood. She had never seen the batches of seed drifting before late May or June, and she wondered what anomaly in the weather had caused them to spread so abundantly, so early in the year.

KIM

ALL OF Kim's fears came true. The worst thing that could happen to a new mother occurred the week before her daughter's first birthday.

She was telling herself she had made it. One of Charles' friends had warned them, "People overcomplicate parenthood. That's where all of the anxiety comes in. Think of it this way: All you have to do is keep your baby alive *for one year*. After that she's on her own. She can stand up and walk away, right? She's got a fighting chance against you."

They'd all laughed. The idea of being a bodyguard for just one year was indeed appealing and comforting. The joke became central to Kim's thinking about the baby. She might be cleaning spit-up off the bassinet, or shopping for disposable diapers, feeling low and tired, and the words would form in her mind. "One year." It became her mantra.

They had moved out of their beloved, funky apartment in a building famous for its 1927 architecture and its annual infestation of mice. They were living in a bright, boxy condo downtown, with a buzzer and a security man to keep out vagrants. All of the appliances were new and tricky to program. The view on sunny days included the tip of the Space Needle and Elliott Bay. Kim didn't say so but sometimes, sitting in her spare, modern living room folding baby clothes and listening to Dido, she felt like she was living in an adult cartoon.

That morning she'd emailed invitations to four other moms. The simple act of designing them and choosing the guest list had reminded her of her isolation, and how much she missed having a real project to occupy her thoughts. Without art she often felt like she was going through the motions of a life.

All of her acquaintances had babies. It was the sole thing they all had in common. Wheeling her daughter through the park in a rain-proof carriage never failed to attract women with a similar mode of travel, women whose Nike jackets were stained with baby formula, whose cheerful yet weary expression signaled: *We're doing our best here. You couldn't do any better. Cut us some slack.*

Once upon a time, she'd admired single-minded artists who shut themselves away in a studio for weeks, emerging only to eat, sleep, and go to the bathroom. Now her circle of heroes included anyone able to keep a strict feeding schedule and still make it to yoga class on time. Her sympathy for these young women sustained her, and they recognized a kindred spirit. They offered practical advice and tips for coping with a world that seldom appreciated their daily sacrifices.

It was a Wednesday. Kim was tired but not exhausted. She was immersed in the kind of fatigue experienced by people who are doing the right thing, no matter how hard it might be. She refused to give up. In another room her baby slept soundly, deeply, after three hours of fussing.

Kim could have fallen asleep on the sofa. For years afterward she would dream of this moment. Visualizing the baby's room she'd just visited two minutes earlier, pulling on a lightweight jacket, choosing an invigorating walk over a quiet nap.

Her favorite café was right around the corner, less than a block away. It occurred to her to call downstairs, to ask Jeff at the front desk if he would step around the corner and buy her a vanilla latte, but the idea made her uneasy.

Jeff was unfailingly friendly and solicitous with her and Charles. What would he think of the privileged mommy with the designer diaper bag who couldn't walk a few hundred feet for a cup of coffee?

She checked the baby again. There were no toys, pillows, or blankets in the bed. The side was up and locked into place. The room temperature was 70 degrees. Nothing could go wrong, and she would be back in less than ten minutes.

She strode from the elevator past the front desk and pretended not to notice when Jeff waved hello. She knew she had a right to go out whenever she wanted. She also knew he was aware of who had entered and exited the building all morning, and would realize she had no babysitter on duty. She dreaded the lighthearted frown, the reminder of her duty, if she had to face Jeff's curiosity. For the past year, no one she knew had ever expected to see her without a carriage or a bundle in her arms. She wondered how many of her neighbors could even recall what she looked like without her daughter.

"The ubiquitous infant," she had once joked to Charles. His reply was a quizzical expression. He simply didn't get her craving for macabre humor.

Once outside, Kim darted left and dodged a homeless man wearing a stocking cap and shabby coat. She trotted to the café, ducked inside, and stepped up to the counter.

"I'd like an iced vanilla latte with crème," she told the barista, whose nose rings vibrated when she spoke.

"The price went up," she said.

"Excuse me?" Kim said.

"Our prices have changed, but we still have the old menu on the wall," said the barista.

"Oh," said Kim. "Okay. Fine." She handed the young woman a ten-dollar bill.

"You don't have a five, do you?" the barista asked.

"What?" Kim said. "No, sorry."

This was followed by an existential sigh from the barista, who proceeded to ring up the order at a cranky vintage cash register. Kim stepped aside to the waiting area, to let another customer place his order. She stood there for five minutes and finally realized the barista wasn't preparing coffee. The young woman had taken three orders in a row without filling them.

"Excuse me," said Kim. "How much longer will it be?"

This infraction of coffee protocol elicited a grim shrug. "We're short a couple of people. I'm supposed to collect three orders at a time, to keep things moving," said the barista.

"But nothing is moving," said Kim. "I've been here for at least ten minutes."

Gray clouds were gathering outside the windows. The sky threatened rain, but this was almost an everyday occurrence.

"I don't think so," said the barista.

"You don't *what?*" Kim asked.

"Look, I'm going as fast as I can. I'm skipping a Reiki workshop to be here."

Now it was Kim's turn to sigh—a deep breath that prompted the barista to roll her eyes. Every movement served to underscore how fed up the young woman was with Kim and people like Kim. She slammed down the handles on the espresso machine and banged a cup on the counter.

"Excuse me," said Kim. "But I ordered mine to go."

"Jesus," the barista said under her breath. "Just a minute."

Two minutes later she delivered a vanilla latte without crème. Kim decided to let it pass. She dropped a quarter in the tip jar to show her contempt and dodged three more customers on her way out.

The sky was gray like pale smoke. The lunchtime rush had begun, and the pavement was crowded with young professionals, tech bros, and homeless people.

She picked up her pace as she rounded the corner. Inside the lobby, she granted Jeff a quick nod. She was home and there was no denying the to-go cup in her hand.

The elevator had never moved so slowly. The trundling motion was maddening. No one else got on or off, yet it seemed to take forever.

Kim reacted to the *ding* of the elevator door signal by sighing with relief. Her adventure was over.

Upon entering the apartment, she placed her coffee on the living room table. Shedding her jacket, she tiptoed across the hall and gently pushed her way into the baby's room.

There was no sound, but this was normal. The lamp on the chest of drawers cast a warmer, gentler glow than the overhead, and she chose it to avoid waking her daughter.

"Emma," she said quietly. When the baby didn't stir, she leaned closer, reached down, and repeated her name. One touch told her everything. There was no movement, not even the birdlike rhythm of an infant breathing.

* * *

In the weeks that followed the death of her child, Kim would take many walks through the neighborhood. She went out two, three, or four times daily.

Nothing mattered. She had no schedule. She quit all other activities in favor of mindless motion, her body pulled along by its own need to move forward. If she stopped even for a minute, the weight of inertia would double her over, a flood of horror overtaking her no matter where she was. She'd never wished for a family, and now the absence of her daughter opened her from the inside out, all of her remaining energy spilling out like blood and viscera.

Charles was grieving, but he had an inner reserve of strength Kim lacked. Maybe it was love, the knowledge that he had wanted and loved their child unconditionally. His desire for a family wasn't vain or trivial; it was his form of faith, a kind of belief in the world itself. Because she didn't share his conviction—that they had done every possible thing to demonstrate love and patience with the most beautiful creature they would ever know—she wasn't only grieving for their loss. She felt shattered, empty of spirit and mind. She mourned for her baby and she mourned for the baby she had chosen not to keep. In their place nothing existed, only bare absence.

They held one another in bed night after night and trembled with the knowledge of what they had lost. Charles was the stronger. He tried to comfort Kim with kind words and reassurances, but every time he reminded her it wasn't her fault, it could have happened to anyone, it was a terrible thing that nevertheless occurred somewhere every day, perhaps every hour—his words only drove her deeper inside, to guilt and shame, to remorse without a chance at redemption.

By the fifth month after the baby died, she was dangerously exhausted. She had given up on therapy and friends. She never left the apartment. The simplest action was beyond her ability. She couldn't predict when or where she'd be when grief would overwhelm her. She broke down in line at the grocery store and left her cart. She began to sob in the middle of an innocuous movie about cheerleaders. One day she dropped to her knees in the park and had to be assisted home by a police officer.

Someone had to do something. With his usual combination of goodwill and determination, Charles insisted on a holiday, a drive down the coast together, with no obligation to enjoy anything or make any progress. He would take the wheel and she could rest or view the sights or just sleep beside him. It was October, the air was clean and bright, and all they wanted was a change of scenery.

TASHA

SINCE THE day they left him lying in the garden outside the cottage, Tyler had become a less distinct memory in a series of more significant events. Tasha hadn't wished him harm. For a couple of days she had worried he might tell the principal or his mom, and there would be hell to pay. Then Tasha spent several days at home while Briar was at the shelter, and when nothing happened, she assumed Tyler was back at school and too cowardly to admit he'd been bullied by a couple of girls.

Then came the dream.

Tasha was walking down the hall at school, looking for Briar. No matter where she searched, there was no sign of her friend. As she rounded a corner, the crowd of students fell away behind her and she could see Tyler heading straight for her.

His chin was tucked in and his forehead loomed, as though he had started growing antlers. A plum-red crescent formed between his eyes, further suggesting horns. His lower lip was curled downward on one side. As he drew near Tasha he scowled, or so she thought. When he passed her, his eyes betrayed a different expression. Not hostility or anger, but an unmistakable look of terror.

She couldn't believe it. She didn't understand it. But she couldn't resist.

"Hey, Tyler," she called out. When he turned she held up both hands, wiggled her fingers, and said, "Boo!"

* * *

"He actually *jumped*," Tasha told Briar on the walk home from school the next day.

"And," said Briar, "this was the end of your dream?"

"Right," said Tasha.

"Nothing more?"

"No," said Tasha. She shifted her weight to balance her backpack. "Why?"

"How do you carry that thing around all day?" Briar asked.

"A backpack?" Tasha asked. "Seriously?"

"A backpack. No. Never mind," said Briar. "I'm kidding."

Tasha regarded her friend with concern. "You know, if you want to talk about what happened, it's okay."

Briar stopped walking. A couple of cars passed. One displayed a bumper sticker that read: *Skillute Will Get You If You Don't Watch Out.*

"Why do you say that?" Briar asked. "Do you think I'm being strange?"

"No. Not really. You're brave. But if you want to tell me anything," said Tasha, "it's okay. I don't mind. I can handle it."

"Do you want me to tell you?" Briar turned to face her. She leaned in close. "Do you want to know the details?"

Something in her expression made Tasha take a step back. That was when she noticed the tattoo again. The tangle of brown leaves and dying vines on Briar's neck had definitely changed since the last time Tasha looked closely. The leaves were fuller than ever, and etched in bright green. And there were tiny buds along the vine, just starting to open at the seams, a white petal barely visible in each one. When she thought about it, Tasha realized Briar had worn a scarf most of the time since she came back from the shelter.

"Your tattoo looks different," she said. "It's—changed."

Briar touched her neck, stroked it with her fingertips. "Do you like it?" she asked. "One of the women at Hope Haven touched it up for me."

Tasha nodded. She didn't say what she was thinking, that this was crazy, that there was absolutely *no way* the people who ran the shelter would have let this happen. But she couldn't imagine how else it occurred. The last time she saw Briar before the fire, the tattoo was brown, the leaves dying. She had been in care, never alone, since then.

"Why don't you believe me?" Briar asked. "What part of my story isn't plausible?"

The word sent a chill through Tasha. She'd been thinking, ever since Briar returned, that her friend was off balance. She didn't sound exactly right. She'd sometimes pause, with her head slightly cocked to one side, before speaking. She didn't look quite right either. Her brown eyes were sharper than before, and somehow they had acquired a gleam, a glint, as though flecked with gold.

"It's plausible," said Tasha. She stopped again at the sound of the word, one that neither of them had used in conversation before. "Why not?" She started walking again.

After a pause Briar joined her. "What's wrong, Tasha?"

"Nothing," she replied. "You've been through a lot. Terrible things change people."

"You think I've changed?" Briar asked. Before Tasha could answer, she said, "I know what you mean. I know. But I can't help it. It's what you said last night, about my mom. I don't know when I'll see my mom again. I'm worried about her."

"My dad says you can visit her if you want to," Tasha said. "He can call and schedule it. Do you want to do that?"

There was the strangely blank expression again, and the slight angle of the head.

"Sure," said Briar. "Yes. I miss her. Why wouldn't I want to see my mother?"

"Okay," said Tasha. "Let's talk to Dad when we get home."

"Hey, do you want to go to the bird cemetery?"

"The what?"

"Our place," said Briar. "I mean your place. The witch's garden." She veered off from the main road, taking the detour to the cottage where they liked to meet.

After a moment, Tasha followed. She didn't know what else to do, and she prayed they wouldn't find Tyler's body, rotting away and utterly forgotten.

* * *

Briar was walking so briskly Tasha couldn't catch up until they reached the gate. Both girls entered and wandered among the broken windmills and birdhouses. There was no sign of Tyler, and nothing to suggest a fight had taken place here.

"You see?" Briar said. "He must have gone home."

"Yeah," said Tasha. "I guess so."

"Now you can stop worrying, and stop dreaming about him," said Briar. "He wasn't worth it."

"You mean 'isn't' worth it," Tasha said.

"Yes, yes," Briar said, an edge of impatience creeping into her voice. "He isn't worth thinking about."

"Why did you call it a bird cemetery?" Tasha asked.

"Children used to come here to try and trap finches and sparrows," said Briar. "They tortured the ones they caught, tore off their wings, and buried them alive in the yard. You see these twigs?" She pointed to a row of sticks close to the fence, barely noticeable unless someone knew where to look. "Tiny graves. Can you hear? Kneel down and listen." She crouched. "Can you hear them crying out, under the ground? Still trying to escape?"

"Briar," said Tasha. When her friend's eyes met her own, they were glistening. "How do you know this? Are you making it up?"

Abruptly Briar stood up and brushed the leaves from her jeans. "Of course," she said. "I made it up. I saw the twigs the other day and started thinking about all the stuff that must have happened here."

"Okay," said Tasha. "Good story."

"There's more to it," said Briar. "But, you know, only if it doesn't frighten you. I heard some good stories in the shelter."

"Okay," said Tasha. She didn't want to make her friend feel awkward. Maybe imagining the history of this place was helping her work through some things.

"The kids who played here were very bad," said Briar. She turned toward Orton and Gretchen, who were leaning together against the fence. "They came from one of the worst families. They went to church every Sunday and said prayers every night because they were afraid. Their people wore crosses around their necks and they gossiped about anyone who was different or strange." She drew closer to Orton and Gretchen. "They were so smug and pious. Fat, hateful, lying, little bastards."

"Briar?" Tasha stood back a few feet, uncertain. Briar was staring at the fence, at nothing, and her voice had climbed until she sounded threatening.

"This is only a story," she told Tasha. "Nothing to worry about. The only ones who need to worry are the nasty children who like to bury things and wait for them to die. The woman who lived in this house found out what they were doing. She caught them one night, digging in her garden. She saw the blood and the broken wings in the wildflowers. Do you know what she did?"

"No," Gretchen whispered.

"What did she do?" Tasha asked.

"No," said Gretchen. "Please." She tried to hide her face against Orton's chest. He was too terrified to speak.

"She lifted them into the air," said Briar. "She held them by the neck and crushed their windpipes so they couldn't scream for help. She threw them onto the ground. She took a spade and cut off their hands and buried them. Right over there!"

Tasha looked to the spot where Briar was pointing. The largest birdhouse in the garden stood there. Tasha had never noticed before, but it was the one structure undamaged by the elements—painted robin egg blue with white trim, sporting several water bottles and feeding trays, which appeared to be full, to the delight of a pair of mourning doves gurgling and helping themselves.

"This is where bad children go," said Briar. "To feed the birds and whisper lies deep down in the dark."

Gretchen and Orton were gone now. Only the doves fluttered above their grave. One of them dropped a thick stream of white shit onto the ground beneath the birdhouse.

KIM

THE GIRLS cleared the table and loaded the dishwasher after dinner. It wasn't a lot, as chores went, but then Charles and Kim had never asked Tasha to do much around the house.

They had a gardening service every other Wednesday. Twice a year they paid a man to power-wash the exterior of the house. Another person stopped by after these cleaning sessions to do the windows. Charles took care of the recycling. Kim tidied up and handled most of the laundry. A Roomba kept the floors free of debris.

Husband and wife sat at the dining table sipping wine. The girls had retired to Tasha's room to play computer games.

"She wants to visit her mother," said Kim.

"Well?" said Charles. "This is a good sign, isn't it? She's back in school and she misses her mom. This is normal. She's coming out of the deep freeze."

"What kind of kid says nothing about her mother, or the fire, or her dead stepdad or whatever he was, for days, and then suddenly announces that she wants to see her mother?" Kim asked.

"She's been through a lot."

"Stop saying that," said Kim, lowering her voice and leaning closer. "Stop being the reasonable one. Tell me the truth, Charles. You see there's something wrong with her, don't you?"

"Honey," he said, also whispering. "You've had reservations about every girl Tasha's ever brought home. No, wait a minute," he said, holding up an index finger to halt her interruption. "You said to tell the truth, and I will. But you have to be honest, too. You've been over-protective and cautious."

"Why wouldn't I be?"

"Because it isn't normal, Kim," he said. "It isn't the way people ought to raise their children. You've kept her too close to you, being her best friend, doing everything she wanted to do just so she would turn to you. Setting her up on play dates with kids and parents you found innocuous."

"Parents with good standards," she said.

"Parents who were too busy hovering over their own kids to notice anything strange," he said.

"Strange?" She gave him a helpless, disappointed expression. "I've done everything possible to help her fit in. You know I have."

"And any time she's made her own choice, you've stopped it," he reminded her.

"I've never stopped her," said Kim.

"No? Her imaginary friend?" he said. "You told her she could call you Tilly. You told her to think of you as both her mom and her invisible friend, combined. What was that all about?"

"It was a phase that went on too long," said Kim. "She needed to outgrow it."

"She was a little girl," he said. "A lonely little girl. And when she hauled a cat home for company, you took it to the animal shelter."

"It scratched her face," said Kim. "She was in danger. Why do you keep bringing this up?"

Charles finished his wine and set the glass on the table. "I'm going to bed," he said. "Tomorrow I'll call Briar's social worker and arrange a visit with her mother."

He left the room. Kim helped herself to another glass, and another. She sat alone for a long time, lost in her thoughts.

BRIAR &
EVELYN

TWELVE MILES from Skillute, the mental health facility where Evelyn Gamel was held offered patients a view of rolling green hills and well-managed gardens dotted with gladiolas. All of this was unavailable to Evelyn, whose agitation at any glimpse of the outside world had prompted her psychiatrist to have her moved to one of the high-security wings. There she spent her time staring at padded walls, sleeping, and reminding anyone who would listen that she had set her husband on fire.

Charles decided it was best if he accompanied the social worker and Briar, leaving Tasha and Kim at home. It was agreed that he would remain in the lobby, the social worker would sign in with Briar, and then the girl would be allowed to speak with Evelyn through a glass partition while a guard kept watch just out of hearing. In this way, all of the adults involved felt they were protecting both the girl and her right to privacy.

There was a blue-white cast to the walls beyond the conventionally decorated lobby. Sound was muffled by insulation throughout.

There were no screams or wails, no patients wandering loose, and no institutional smells. All was clean, muted, and calm. In the wing where Evelyn resided, a second lobby allowed visitors a chance to be seated, to help themselves to water in paper cups, and to reflect more or less privately while waiting for an orderly to bring the patient from her room.

"Briar Gamel," the receptionist intoned when all was ready.

The social worker helped to usher Briar down the hall and into a small booth equipped with a plastic chair, a small countertop, and a window perforated with holes for sound. She nodded encouragingly and then stepped outside, leaving Briar to face the haggard woman on the other side of the glass.

Evelyn stared at the countertop. Her skin was dry, her lips chapped. Her hair hung loose about her shoulders. She was wearing a white T-shirt over boxy cotton trousers with an elastic waist. When she finally looked at Briar, it was without a flicker of recognition. Her daughter might have been a fly or a light fixture.

Briar gazed up overhead and followed the line where the ceiling met the wall. For some reason she was feeling lightheaded, her thoughts a bit clouded as if filtered through gauze. It was hard to distinguish what was real and what was bleeding through reality. She considered the gaunt, middle-aged woman on the other side of the safety glass.

"Do you like it here?" she asked.

Evelyn said nothing. She didn't appear to have heard the question.

"Is this better than prison?" Briar asked. This time, when Evelyn didn't answer, she sighed. "Enough about you, then," she said. "Do you know this is the first time I've been outside of Skillute in, oh, at least seventy years? Imagine that."

Evelyn's head shimmied ever so slightly. Her eyes remained dull and unfocused.

"I admit, it feels strange," said Briar. "Sort of like floating. Think what it must be like to lie underground, feeling the beat of people passing, trucks and cars, children playing, animals burrowing up close to your lips, sleeping in your hair! And you can't speak, can't move. All you can do is lie there in the cold darkness, dreaming of setting the world on fire."

Now Evelyn's eyes fixed upon Briar. She opened her mouth as if to reply, but no words came.

"Your daughter is perfect, you know," said Briar. "Her skin is young and smooth. She's coming into her own at the right time. No one will tell her to be silent and take her medicine. No one will turn her into a thing, a vessel for other things. If they try, she has every right to harm them. She *will* harm them. She's killed a man and might do it again. She's exquisite."

"Who are you?" Evelyn asked. Her voice, so seldom used, had become a rasping whisper. She pursed her lips and squinted at Briar. "Who are you?"

Briar ran her fingertips over her neck and felt the raw contours of her tattoo. She was having trouble concentrating, and it annoyed her to realize this was because she was away from home. She had anticipated a sense of freedom.

"Mother, dear," said Briar. "Don't embarrass yourself, and don't hurt my feelings. I've come all this way to visit with you. Don't you recognize me?"

"Fire," said Evelyn. "Ray, crawling, in the fire."

"You do remember that part," said Briar. "Did you see his face— the skin blackened and torn, the muscles contorting underneath? He was howling. Remember that part, Evvy—Ray-Ray on his hands and knees, trying to drag himself outside? He was howling and crying at the same time until his vocal chords dried up, and then he could only lie there whimpering. What a sight. He urinated so much I was afraid he might put out the fire!"

"This isn't my child," said Evelyn. "Give back my girl."

"You're not fit to raise a child, Evelyn. Don't you know that?"

"Find my girl," said Evelyn. "Where is she? Find her! Find her or I'll kill you!"

Briar watched the distraught woman with a new gleam of curiosity in her eyes. She put her face closer to the glass.

"My baby," said Evelyn. "It's your fault, you bastard!"

"Who?" Briar asked. "Who is it?"

"Fred, you fucking bastard!" Evelyn said. "I don't believe anything you say. You gave her away for a fucking half a gram!"

Briar smiled. This was more than she ever expected. "Who is Fred?"

"I killed him," said Evelyn. She was starting to cry. "I killed my husband. It was me."

"Yes," said Briar. "You killed your husband."

"Fred," said Evelyn.

"Ray," said Briar. "Rayburn Kenny."

"He was a liar," Evelyn said. "He stole my child."

Briar observed the soft shadows under the woman's eyes. "Poor Evvy," she said. "I have a new life now. They say it's temporary, but I'll find a way. I haven't struggled all of these years just to give up. Poor, poor, old Evelyn! You look terrible. Ray would hate your clothes. But he's dead. He's a bag of ashes in a tiny box. They'll FedEx him to his fat sister in Spokane—the one he was always talking about—and she'll tell her friends he was a famous musician who died too young. Her friends will believe her, because people are stupid. Oh well. Time to go."

Evelyn's eyes widened. She studied Briar's face. "Who are you?" she said. "Who are you?"

* * *

"I'm so sorry," the social worker said. "I was hoping for a good outcome."

"What would that be?" Briar asked. She touched her forehead. The gauzy sensation was gone and he was beginning to feel real pain now. If they didn't return to Skillute soon, she didn't know what might happen.

They stood with Charles on the pavement in front of the hospital. Two abstract sculptures decorated the space on either side of them. Both adults hung their heads, unable to offer much comfort to the girl in their care.

"Anything would have been an improvement. If she doesn't connect with her own daughter," said the social worker, "I'm afraid she hasn't made any progress."

"I think she's worse," said Briar. She looked at them both and shrugged. She was trying to control her foul mood. She watched two dead women walk from the hospital to the parking lot, their arms linked. One of the women had a thin scar that ran across her neck from ear to ear. It made Briar smile.

"I'm sorry," Charles said. He put a hand on her shoulder. The social worker offered Briar an awkward hug before she left.

As they pulled out of the parking lot and headed home, Charles added, "It must be hard to see your mother like this."

"She's always been a little bit crazy," said Briar. "Always telling stories, you know, making things up. But she was funny, too. Now she's just—not really there."

They passed an overturned cart. Logs had tumbled onto the road, pinning and crushing a man who wore overalls. A crowd was gathering around the man.

Charles glanced at Briar, but she didn't seem upset, only curious. He tried to maneuver around the accident as quickly as possible.

"Well," said Charles, "you've got us, for as long as you need us. You've got Tasha and Kim and me."

Briar flashed her best smile, brave and sweet. At least, she hoped he would see it that way. She'd been practicing all morning. "Thanks," she said. "I'm okay. Let's go home."

* * *

Two interns had to help remove Evelyn from the booth and guide her back to her room. There she grew quiet, although her memories, broken as they were, fed her white-hot images, one after another. What she remembered kept colliding with what she imagined. It felt as if her brain were overloaded, crackling, and threatening to break through her skull.

Back then she had her own name, her real name. Evelyn was something she made up. Gamel was a lie, too. She was born Julie Dodd, but she would bury her name and the town where she lived in Oregon, and the reason she had to leave.

Fred Morrow had been a master carpenter by trade. He was lean and strong, with beautiful hands. He could build almost anything. He was estranged from his family and said he'd never been able to get along with his mother. He called her 'a ridiculous woman.' This probably should have been a warning sign, but Julie chose to ignore it.

When he wasn't constructing furniture, Fred grew restless. He calmed down with beer and weed, but these were poor substitutes. As Julie discovered, his great love was heroin.

"You don't want to see this guy when he can't get his hands on a half gram," one of Fred's friends joked.

Even after she knew this, she wanted him. And now, after all these years, she could still conjure the taste of copper and salt in his sweat. Julie would get down on her knees to unbutton his trousers, work clothes crusted with paint and sawdust, and take him in her mouth. With any other man, she would have made excuses to stop when she felt he was about to ejaculate. Fred's come was like warm mineral water on her tongue, and she swallowed without hesitation. When he wasn't in the room with her, even if he was only downstairs or on his way home, she burned with jealousy and the need to see his face and brush her fingers through his dark hair.

Julie was studying cosmetology. All of her classmates told her she was crazy to stay with Fred. If those people only knew!

"You're really going to marry Fred?" His best friend asked her this a week before they walked to the courthouse downtown for a civil ceremony, followed by saké and a platter of sushi at a real restaurant.

"You know he's fucked up, right? Not in a cool way. There's something wrong with his brain cells."

She didn't know. She didn't want to know. All of her life she had acted on impulse, never planning or preparing. She called it 'following her heart.' Her father had called it 'following her snatch,' the night he'd kicked her out of the house for good.

For almost a year Fred went out of his way to please her. Their days and nights together were the happiest times she'd ever known. They drank too much, ate too much, and laughed at how miserable other people were compared to them. She learned to cook lasagna and spaghetti with homemade sauce. He bought a lathe and spent hours building and restoring furniture to fill the fixer-upper they leased from a retired teacher.

They were browsing at a block-long garage sale the day he blew up at her for the first time. She was three months pregnant and feeling sick. She took a detour while Fred bargained with a man in a wheelchair over a useless set of antiquated optical testing equipment.

Julie asked a woman sitting on the porch next door if she could have a glass of water. The woman invited her in. The women were gone no more than two or three minutes. When they emerged, Julie found Fred stomping back and forth on the sidewalk, swinging his arms in an exaggerated way. Before she could reach him he cupped both hands in front of his mouth and bellowed her name.

"Here!" she shouted. "I'm right here, Fred!"

He came barreling toward her with such speed and intent, she thought for a moment that he was going to strike her. It was like nothing she'd ever seen before, comical as a cartoon, but she was afraid to laugh.

"Where the fuck have you been?" he yelled.

"I just went inside for a drink of water," she explained.

"Why? Why the hell would you do that, Julie?" He was getting louder every time he spoke. The people gathered around the sales tables and furniture were growing quiet, surreptitiously observing.

Julie's face felt hot. She wasn't absolutely sure he wouldn't hit her. He'd never shouted at her in public like this, and she was still trying to get her bearings. The thought of violence made her both frightened and ashamed of being frightened. It crossed her mind that the crowd of strangers was waiting for her to do something, or say something, but she didn't know what would calm him, or what might make things worse. She had never seen him so angry.

"Anything could have happened to you!" he shouted. "Do you know that? Do. You. Understand. You could *disappear* and what the fuck am I supposed to do?"

"It's all right," she said meekly. "I'm fine."

"It's fucking irresponsible!"

"It's okay, Fred."

"If this is the way you act, you just wander off and disappear, how are you going to take care of anybody?" he yelled. "How can you be a mother?"

She felt a drop, a sensation of falling, inside. She was humiliated but too stunned to cry or to argue. She was trying to think what else she could say to defend her actions, when he spun around and started walking away.

She could feel all of the strangers watching her. She couldn't meet their gaze. Fred was storming off, down the street, toward the car. If she didn't catch up to him, he might leave her stranded. She was broke. The garage sales were nothing but a distraction on a hot day. This was how they passed the time when they couldn't afford to go anywhere.

She started walking faster. Her new weight prevented her from breaking into a run, so she trotted, aware that she looked ridiculous, like a child made to scurry to avoid being left behind.

He never apologized. He brought home roses stolen from a neighbor's yard, and a bottle of Belgian ale. He cried and held her in bed and pressed his ear close to her abdomen to listen, but he didn't say he was sorry.

* * *

The next two years changed Julie forever. She knew it, experienced it in her bones and her blood, in the very chemistry of her body. Fred never hit her, but when he was raging she sat still and quiet, paralyzed by fear. Her fear had become a constant. She said nothing. Afterward she drank beer to dull her memory of all he'd said to her while his brain was on fire.

She went on living with him. She ignored the advice of people who knew him. She found work at a salon, sweeping up and taking reservations. She said nothing every time he quit a good job because some guy pissed him off. She came home from happy hour drinks with a co-worker and found him 'swimming' in the wild grass in the back yard, a needle tossed carelessly aside.

The outside of their house remained unpainted, and dandelions sprouted in the yard. The owner, the retired teacher with a Canadian accent, warned them she would have to evict if they ruined the property, yet she never failed to help out when they were stuck for a babysitter.

Fred said the woman was an asshole. He also said he could 'maintain,' and he was 'able to function,' but he never painted the house or cleaned up the yard. Julie accepted all of his demands and explanations while her desire for him faded silently, daily.

Finally the disaster came, and all of it was Julie's fault. She had thought about this in every way possible, forward and backward, for twelve years. She never shook the conviction that she'd caused all of it.

She stayed late at work that day. Not because she had to, but because she wasn't ready to go home. She wasn't in the mood to wade through the scratchy weeds and tall yellow grass, or to see Fred's face when she walked through the door. The minute she arrived, he would give up all responsibility as the designated babysitter and run off to perform one of his 'errands.'

She was finishing up the final shift. She cleaned up the front desk, and helped a new girl sweep up the hair on the floor. Afterward she locked the doors and flipped the cardboard sign. Her boss, a loud and brassy woman everyone called Babs, put her feet up and offered Julie a bottle of beer.

No one at work knew anything about her life at home. She never introduced Fred to her co-workers at the salon. They all knew she drank too much, but they had troubles of their own. They didn't ask, and she didn't offer any sob stories.

It was a Saturday, and that meant Fred would be meeting his 'guy' in a parking lot somewhere. They would give one another a signal, and Fred would follow him into a public bathroom to exchange cash for a half gram.

Until Julie got home, he'd have to watch TV and keep an eye on the kids. If he absolutely had to go out, he could ask the landlady to babysit for an hour.

Julie having twins was the last thing they had expected. When the sonogram revealed their future, Fred acted confused, like he had been tricked.

"What makes you think we can afford two kids?" he asked, as if she'd planned it all without his permission.

Now it was fall, the weather was changing, and Julie was tired. She worked hard. She didn't want to rush home from the salon. She accepted a bottle of beer from her boss, and put her feet up. Fred could wait.

Only, as it turned out, he couldn't wait. He had the jitters. He made a call to tell his guy he'd be late, and the guy said he would only be around for another half hour, forty-five minutes tops.

As Fred tried to explain to Julie when he finally returned home, realizing he was going to miss his connection made him break into a sweat. He had paced and waited, and paced some more. When Julie didn't show up at her usual time, or after another fifteen minutes, he had called the babysitter, but she didn't answer. So he did the only thing he could think of, the only thing that made sense.

He grabbed the kids. He strapped them into the back seat, one singing a stupid song from a TV commercial, the other falling asleep. He drove like a bat out of hell to the McDonald's on 14th Street. He went in, ordered fries, and gave a few to the kids to keep them quiet. He locked the car and ran back inside.

He was sure, he said later, he had locked the car. He was absolutely sure. So what happened wasn't really his fault, he said. He didn't do anything wrong. He did everything he was supposed to do. He didn't know what the fuck Julie wanted him to do about it. He'd already driven around the neighborhood for over an hour, hunting, and the only thing left was to go to the police, which he couldn't do for obvious reasons. If he called the cops, they'd ask around at McDonald's, and who knew if a witness had seen part of his transaction in the bathroom? He could go to prison, and Julie would be alone. Worse, his guy could get arrested and then his guy would definitely have Fred killed.

"So what the hell more could I do?" he asked, his voice climbing. "What the fuck do you want me to do?"

Julie sat on the couch in shock, her mouth open, her life shattered. Her baby was sitting on the floor, playing with wooden blocks.

Fred asked her again what the fuck she wanted him to do about it. Then he turned away and stared out the window with his hands on his hips, as if he'd tried everything a man could possibly do before giving up.

She could have said, "Nothing, as usual. Do nothing, Fred, because you're a shiftless piece of human trash." But she was too busy to say these things. She was in motion.

First she stood up. Then she picked up the ceramic ashtray that had been sitting on the living room table for two years. She grasped it in both hands and smashed it into the back of his head. When he plummeted to the floor, she hit him again.

She would have ended her story—if she'd ever told it to anyone—by saying she ran and never looked back, but that would be a lie. Her whole life was looking back at that day, at Fred, unconscious, bleeding wildly into a threadbare rug, and her only child screaming on the floor.

The baby was still screaming, in the back seat, ten minutes later when Julie slammed the car into reverse and backed out of the driveway for the last time. She went mad that day. It was the last time she was able to concentrate on one thing specifically and clearly. She drove from her house to McDonald's, to the shopping mall, to every vacant lot and park. She knew it was hopeless searching for a child in this way, but she couldn't stop.

Again and again, she followed the same route until she was exhausted. The baby had cried herself to sleep in the back seat. Hysteria gradually gave way to a numb realization that she had killed Fred and her only chance at keeping her only daughter was to get out of there, take the freeway exit, and flee.

She would have chosen to never look back, to lose the person she'd become under the weight of her life with Fred. She would try to lose it, every day, with Briar. But the sickening thing was, every moment with her daughter reminded her of the one who was lost, the twin Briar had obviously forgotten. Later on, with every drink and every night she spent with Ray, she tried to outrun the past, but nothing worked. She could never get away. The thing she wanted to let go of was her own soul.

* * *

In the relative safety of her hospital room, Evelyn raised her head from the cot. It was time for oblivion. The nurse offered a thin smile along with a dose of clozapine to take the monsters away.

TASHA & BRIAR

"WHAT WAS it like?" Tasha asked.

"Talking with my psychotic mother?" Briar asked. "It was great fun. Wish I could do it every day for breakfast."

"I'm sorry. Is that the diagnosis? She's psychotic?"

"Yeah, I guess so," said Briar. "She's very confused. She didn't even recognize me."

"Shit," said Tasha. "That's terrible."

"Is it?" Briar asked. Her head was clearing, her thoughts becoming more distinct, now that she was on familiar ground again. "Oh. That's too bad."

"My grandmother has Alzheimer's," Tasha told her. "My mom says it's the worst thing in the world, when your own mom doesn't recognize you. It's like you don't really exist." She stopped. "I'm sorry, Briar. That's awful. Who knows? Maybe the medication will help her. Do they think she might get better?"

"If she does improve, I think they'll take her out of the hospital and send her to prison," said Briar. "She committed murder."

"Are they sure?" Tasha asked.

"Why would you say that?" Briar was peering at her with one of those expressions Tasha found hard to read.

"Have they found evidence? I mean they can't just take the word of someone who's mentally ill, can they?" Tasha said. "And why would she murder him? You said they were in love. There's no motive."

"Well," said Briar, "as you put it: Who knows? Two people are together and in love and then one of them wants to leave. Or one of them meets someone else. Or I don't know. A million things."

"You believe she did it on purpose?" Tasha asked. "She set fire to the place where she lived and paid rent, where you were sleeping, to kill a guy when she could just throw him out? It doesn't seem strange to you?"

Briar hung her head in exasperation. She wanted to lie down, to give in to the buzzing of her beautiful thoughts. It was such a slow, painful job talking to people. She mumbled, "Everything's strange, Tasha. My whole life is wrecked unless I can find a permanent place to stay. Think about that. I don't know Ray's family at all, and if they made *him*, I don't think I want to live with them."

Tasha put an arm around Briar and hugged her. They sat together like this, leaning on the edge of Tasha's bed, for a while.

Tasha was ashamed of her unkindness. All this time her friend was suffering, trying to be brave, and all Tasha could think about was how she didn't act the right way or say the right things.

"Hey, listen," said Tasha at last. "I want to give you something."

She went to the dresser and rummaged through one of the drawers, scattering underwear, socks, and scarves. At last she found what she wanted. "This isn't expensive or anything but I've had it all of my life, as far as I remember. I guess it's known me longer than any other thing I own. Here, I want you to have it."

She opened her palm to reveal a slender silver bracelet with a sliding lock, engraved with the initial B. "You should keep it, anyway," she said. "Since your name starts with a B." She smiled.

"Where did you find this?" Briar asked with her head cocked to one side.

"My mom bought it at a vintage shop in Seattle before I was born."

"Is that what she told you?" Briar asked coldly.

"Yeah," said Tasha, taken aback by her friend's tone of voice. "She was expecting me, and she saw this in the window of a little store she liked. She was deciding what my name would be, and that day she was thinking: Bettina. Then she saw the bracelet and she bought it."

"Your name isn't Bettina." Again there was that coldness, and Briar's eyes flashed and glinted with gold flecks.

"No," said Tasha. "Later on, she changed her mind. But she liked the bracelet, and she gave it to me when I was two or three. I wore it for years. It doesn't fit anymore, but it's pretty and I want you to have it." She took Briar's hand, turned it over, and placed the bracelet in her palm.

Briar stared at the silver band with her initial engraved in it. She rubbed her thumb against the lock and everything clicked. "Blair," she said. She handed the bracelet back to Tasha. "That was your name. Don't you remember? Blair! A toddler with a serious expression, biding your time in the back seat, waiting for your real father to return! Remember!" She placed a hand on Tasha's face.

Tasha couldn't move. A rush of sensations ran through her at the sound of the name. The images in her head, long set aside and forgotten through neglect, began to flicker: the dark gray beaches and the sea tinged with white froth; black clouds gliding over the rocks; the road and the fog; a porch dotted with jack o' lanterns; and someone leaning into the car, a silhouette reaching toward her, unbuckling the seatbelt...

"What's wrong?" Briar asked, smiling.

"Sick. I'm going to be sick," said Tasha.

She bolted out of the bedroom and across the hall. The sound of her retching brought Kim running from her office. She went to

Tasha, rubbed her back and shoulders. She ran a washrag under the tap, wrung it out, and held the cold compress to the back of Tasha's neck.

"What's the matter, baby?" Kim asked. "Where does it hurt?"

"Mom," the girl mumbled. She began to shiver and cry. "Mom!"

Kim washed her daughter's face, smoothed her hair, and held her in her arms on the bathroom floor. She'd done this many times over the years, and they always sat like this, mother cradling child and whispering words of comfort until she lay quiet and calm.

Behind them, Briar shook her head. It was all too much, the noise and the heat of emotions, the rush of words, all of them transparent and false. Adults could do this, lie through their teeth, and get away with it.

* * *

Later, with Tasha tucked into bed, Kim called Charles at work to ask if he could come home early. "I didn't see how it started," Kim said into the phone. "I know you're trying to catch up at the office, but I need you. Okay. I'll be waiting." She hung up. She checked on Tasha one last time.

When she walked into the living room she still had the phone in her hand. She saw Briar standing at the window.

Kim sat down wearily. The girl turned to face her, and she seemed taller than before, etched against the glass that ran the length of the room.

"Is she going to be all right?" the girl asked.

"She'll be fine," said Kim. "Can you tell me what happened?"

"Don't you know?" Briar asked.

Kim reached forward and placed the bracelet on the coffee table. "She was holding this. I don't know why."

"Do you want to talk about it, Kim?" Briar asked.

"I think it's time we had a talk about your future."

"Oh," said Briar. "You want me to go away?"

"I'm sorry," Kim told her. "But it would be best for everyone."

Briar took a step toward her. "Best for *me*?"

"You might not see it now," said Kim. "But in the long run, yes, I think you'll be happier with your own people."

Briar shrugged. She tilted her head at an odd angle. "Who are my people, Kim?"

"Just because your mother never told you about her family doesn't mean there isn't one, somewhere. And what about your biological father?"

Behind Briar, the overcast sky spread across the wall like a canvas. Bits of cottonwood drifted on air, delicate as snowflakes.

"Haven't you heard, Kim?" Briar asked. "Haven't you been paying attention? Oh, no, of course not. Only I know. I remember it very well, now. Evelyn killed my father. Or at least, she thinks she did. Who knows? Maybe there's a man with a beard full of lice eating from a trash dumpster in an alley somewhere in Portland or Seattle right now, wondering why his wife tried to murder him twelve years ago. Would you be able to identify him, Kim? Would you come with me to every shelter and hospital, to search for him?"

"What makes you think I would recognize him?" Kim's voice cracked and betrayed her. Briar noticed at once, and before Kim could speak again the girl stepped forward and picked up the bracelet. She held it up in the light and turned it over.

"This," Briar said. "She tried to give this to me as a gift." She cocked her head to one side. "You recognize it, don't you, Kim?"

Now Kim's eyes went dull. She stared at the bracelet as Briar drew near.

"Where did she find this?" Kim asked.

"Tasha was keeping it safe in her room," said Briar. "I had one—Briar had one—just like it, so long ago she had almost forgotten. See this tiny scar, on her wrist?" She held up her arm. "Briar cut her skin trying to work the lock, and her mother threw the bracelet away. She forgot all about it. Until we saw this one, the one Blair was wearing the day she disappeared."

"No," said Kim, her voice wavering. "What are you saying? *You're* Briar. You're mistaken. You're confused."

"No, not any more. You're so confused, Kim. You're lying. You've been lying for such a long time it probably feels like the truth. I understand. I'm a liar, too."

"You've been through a terrible ordeal," said Kim. Though she tried to steady herself, her hands were shaking and tears began coursing down her face. "You don't know what you're talking about."

"You've done something bad, Kim," Briar said, and her voice was deeper and more distinct than ever. "Something worse than murder. One of the worst things a woman can do."

"No…" Kim sputtered.

Briar drew closer. "Denial won't help you now."

"No!"

"No! You're so much worse than a murderer, Kim," said Briar. "So much worse."

"Please," Kim cried. "Please don't take my daughter!"

"Your daughter?" Briar asked. She shook her head and laughed. "Oh no, she isn't the one I want. What good would it do, to occupy another adolescent girl?"

"What?" Kim was shivering with fear and confusion. "What do you want?"

"Let me show you," said Briar.

Kim sprang to her feet and tried to rush past Briar. But the girl caught her, both hands on Kim's neck, forcing her down. When she fell into a seated position on the sectional, Briar climbed onto her lap, knees flanking her and holding her in place. Kim struggled to breathe and Briar leaned closer, pressing their foreheads together, grimacing, staring straight down into her eyes.

KIM

IT WAS October, but in her grief and depression Kim barely noticed the season. Charles kept pointing out houses with pumpkins on the front porch and in the yard, but not the ones decorated with plastic skeletons and paper ghosts shivering in the breeze.

From their starting point in Seattle, they followed the Oregon Coast Highway south. Charles had loaded the car with maps and guidebooks. They took their time, following any detour of interest, stopping to eat when they were hungry, checking into a bed and breakfast or motel to rest when they found a vacancy.

They were in no hurry. Charles had accrued too many vacation days at work. He'd been told, in a polite and thoughtful way, to use them or lose them. He was devoting his full attention to Kim and her needs. Nothing else mattered.

They rented an overnight bungalow near Long Beach. There they drank wine in the Jacuzzi, ate oysters, slept late, and took a long walk. They stopped at Marsh's Free Museum and said hello to Jake the Alligator Man. Charles put a coin in the penny press and made a souvenir for Kim to keep in her wallet.

They followed the highway out to the jagged black rocks of the coast and back inland through farmlands and rivers. They visited the *Peter Iredale* shipwreck, the lonesome hull sticking out of the sand like the spine of an ancient beast picked clean by the elements.

In Astoria they ate at a funky little diner called the Dropp Inn. Charles was pleased to see Kim's appetite renewed by travel. They devoured cheeseburgers and fries and split a plate of onion rings. In the afternoon they watched the sun slip across the bridge, and took photos of the river.

The southernmost point of the trip was Sisters Rocks in Oregon. Here the dark gray sand had a deep undercurrent of purple, and the isolated black peaks were surrounded by smaller and smaller stacks, traveling outward from the land like an echo.

On the last day before they headed back north to Seattle, Kim offered her first suggestion of the entire trip. She wanted to drive inland again, find a dumpy little town, and buy a vanilla milkshake at McDonald's.

"What if the dumpy little town doesn't have a McDonald's?" Charles said, smiling.

"Every dumpy little town has at least one," Kim said, not quite smiling but nearly, nearly. "Who knows? There might be one on every corner."

Charles chose the freeway exit at a place called Midas. He drove east, and soon they were engulfed in the familiar sights of a generic American town. They passed a barbershop where two old men sat out front reading newspapers. Nearby a pack of skateboarders practiced heelflips. In the background, the local Walmart loomed like the Taj Mahal.

"How much real estate is that?" Kim asked.

"About a hundred thousand square feet," said Charles, happy to make small talk. "A superstore would be double that."

At the next intersection they spied golden arches. Charles headed north to a mainly residential street and pulled into the parking lot. "What do I win?" he asked.

"My admiration," said Kim.

"Do you want drive-through, or shall we join the hoi polloi indoors?"

"Oh," said Kim, "I think the classy approach is to enjoy our shakes in the luxury of our vehicle, don't you?"

"Back in two minutes," he said.

The place looked busy, but not crazy busy. Some people ate in cars, some at the picnic tables by the side of the building. The playground with its red plastic slide was empty.

Kim let her seat back a couple of inches and relaxed. She had to admit, the trip was a good idea. The dull routine of her days in Seattle had taken her deeper into a numb state of mind where nothing seemed to matter. Change, movement, different sights flashing by, had begun to bring her back.

Most of the cars in the lot were older and more beat-up than hers. She thought of all the people working for an hourly wage in this misnamed town, treating themselves to an early dinner of fast food. If she'd had to live there, she would have called it a dump. As a visitor she could afford to be generous, but the houses and cars really were rundown.

Charles had been gone a few minutes, not the two he promised, when Kim was distracted by an odd exchange. A gruff, bearded man who'd been waiting by the entrance gave a nod as another man, wearing dirty jeans and a ripped T-shirt, approached him. The man in the dirty jeans had climbed out of a car parked a few spaces away from Kim.

She watched the two men enter McDonald's, but they didn't appear to be together. There was just the one slight signal between them. In a yard across the street some children were playing with a dog, tossing a ball in the air and cheering when the dog, a golden retriever, leapt up and caught it.

Kim's attention drifted back to the car vacated by the man in dirty jeans. Strapped into the back seat was a toddler. A moment later the man came out of the restaurant with a pack of French fries.

He took these to the car, and gave what looked like a handful of fries to the toddler. Then he went back indoors.

A few more minutes passed. Kim kept an eye on the toddler, and her mind raced with the possible horrors of life with a negligent dad. Maybe he was tired. Maybe he was out of work. But leaving a child unattended in a parking lot was crazy. Anything could happen. As if to underscore this, a man in a shabby suit walked by, on the sidewalk, pushing a grocery cart full of plastic bags and glass bottles. The bottles clinked together every time he took a step.

At last Charles emerged with a paper cup in each hand. He smiled when he saw Kim. He crossed the parking lot and climbed in behind the steering wheel.

"Here you go," he said. "Sorry it took so long. You won't believe what I just saw."

Kim sipped her shake. She kept her eyes on the toddler.

"I had to take a leak," said Charles. "That's why I was in there for a while."

"Okay."

"Guess what I saw go down in the men's bathroom?" he asked.

"'Go down,'" she repeated. "What do you mean?"

"A good old-fashioned drug deal," he said. "Reminded me of my youth. Remember those bathroom stalls at the Broadway Market?"

Kim turned to him. "A drug deal?"

"Yes," he said. "In broad daylight."

"You mean they smoked a joint?"

"Oh no," said Charles. "This was for real. They're probably still there. I got the hell out."

"Who was it?" she asked. "What did they look like? Was it a guy with a beard and another guy in ratty jeans?"

"Yeah," he said. "Why?"

She didn't hear him. She was out of the car and dashing toward another vehicle.

"Kim?" he called out, but she ignored him.

She wasn't at all surprised to find the car door unlocked. She opened it and leaned in, her rain jacket making a crinkling sound. She didn't know what she intended. She could have stayed there until the man came out, and lectured the man on how precious children are and how you can never take your eyes off of them for a minute. But the story of the men exchanging money and drugs in the bathroom had flipped some internal switch, and she couldn't stop.

She reached in, loosened the straps of the seatbelt, and lifted the child into her arms. It was only then, as she was backing out the door, that she realized the bundle next to the toddler was another child, a sleeping child who groaned and rubbed a tiny fist against its face, and then for one sharp, terrible instant looked directly at Kim. She felt her heartbeat, a hard thud between her ribs, an ache she couldn't stop. It was as though they were the only people alive in the world. The moment Kim broke away, she might as well have killed the child she left behind. She knew she would spend the rest of her days trying to escape, but she had no choice. She had done the most terrible thing imaginable, and it was time to run.

"What are you doing?" Charles twisted around in the driver's seat while Kim placed the child in back and fastened the seatbelt. "What the hell are you doing?"

"Drive," she told him. "Drive, Charles, or we're fucked."

The next second seemed like a lifetime. Prior to it, their world had come to a crashing halt; on the other side of it lay an eternity of lies. He saw the brightness in Kim's eyes, an alert readiness he hadn't seen in months. He saw the light and dark patterns behind her eyes, a sort of madness folded into reverence. It was the reason he had fallen in love with her, married her, longed to have a family with her. He saw her watching the door of the restaurant with apprehension, and he knew he had no more time to consider what to do. He started the engine, pulled out of the parking lot in one smooth curve, and headed up the street toward the freeway entrance.

* * *

They knew it was insane. By the time they reached Eugene they were nearly hysterical.

Charles chose a two-story motel behind a Chinese restaurant. There was barely any traffic. He checked in at the manager's office, signed the register beneath the red glow of the neon sign, and then drove around the building to their assigned room. He retrieved their bags from the trunk while Kim carried the child inside. As soon as the door was locked and curtains closed, he collapsed into a chair.

"What are we doing, Kim? Jesus Christ. What the hell are we doing?"

"Take a deep breath," she said. "Don't frighten her."

"A girl?" he asked. "She's a girl? God. Oh god. What did we do?"

The steadiness of Kim's voice surprised him. Now that they were no longer in motion, she was composed.

"We rescued a baby from a terrible life with a junky," she said sweetly to the child, who gazed up at her with brown eyes and grinned. "You see, Charles? She knows who we are."

"Who are we?" he asked.

"The parents of a beautiful little girl. Yes, darling. Forever and ever."

"How can we do this?" he asked. "The police will put out an alert."

"Maybe," she said.

"Maybe?"

"You saw that guy," she said. "Did he look like someone who'd run to the nearest police station? I doubt if he has a current photo."

"You've been thinking this over."

"Enough to guess he won't circulate his story," she said.

"What about surveillance?" he said. "CCTV?"

"At a fast food place, probably not," she said. "But even if they have a camera, they won't check the footage unless someone reports an incident."

"Incident?" He watched her gently drumming her fingertips on the toddler's belly, eliciting another grin. "It's kidnapping."

"We saw a child in danger and we stepped in," she said.

"Listen," he said. "Have you been…you haven't had this in mind all along, have you?"

Kim turned to Charles. Her expression told him she was genuinely shocked by the question.

"This is a once-in-a-lifetime miracle," she said. "This little girl needed us and we were there. Don't analyze it, Charles. Accept this, accept her, as a gift."

With this Kim scooped up the girl, who was beginning to grow drowsy again. She placed the child in his arms. He held her, the tiny face with rosebud mouth and delicate eyelashes inches from his face. He was gone, as Kim knew he would be, fallen in love all over again. She would never tell him about the other child, the one she'd left behind. He needed to believe they had done something good, something true, or he would never go along with it.

This was the family he longed for with every cell in his body. His baby had been taken, and as much as he tried, he couldn't help feeling it was unfair for decent people to suffer while a beautiful child was left to the care of an irresponsible and dangerous man. He held his daughter in his arms while Kim went to the Chinese restaurant and bought takeout, including wonton soup and rice for their hungry daughter.

* * *

Once they reached Seattle, they had to form a more detailed plan. This involved putting Kim up in a motel in Bellingham for a week while Charles let a few choice words slip about adoption. They had been on a list for months, and had become discouraged, but then good news had arrived. If they were willing to take a two-year-old rather than wait for an infant, there was a glimmer of hope.

They only shared this news with the friends they couldn't avoid.

They sidestepped all specific questions—what agency they had used, whether they knew the child's birth mother. They explained that they'd done a lot of research and were considering not telling Tasha she was adopted. They swore their close friends to secrecy. But there were meddlers, helpers, friends who couldn't keep their advice and opinions to themselves.

When it became clear that they'd never be able to trust every adult in their daughter's life, they decided to move. They found the dullest, most innocuous-sounding spot with decent schools, a town where they could afford a nice home. They left the city behind and let their old friends drift away.

MRS. TED
VAN DEVERE

SHE PARKED her car on the road in front of the Davis house and hesitated. She had noticed for several days that the air was filled with cottonwood fibers, much too early in the season. This in itself was a sign, but she had yet to determine the meaning. She tried to locate the source by divining. She meditated and traveled in her sleep. She searched Skillute and all the surrounding area, but found no answer.

One thing Mrs. Ted Van Devere knew for certain was that Briar Kenny was no longer the girl who had shared a trailer with her awful parents. Her conversation with the girl wasn't entirely conclusive. She might have been mentally disturbed or acting out.

Since that day, Mrs. Ted Van Devere had done some snooping. She learned that the person known as Briar Kenny had taken up residence, as she wished, with the Davis family. And her night travels had convinced her that this match would be destructive. Not only to this family, but possibly to everyone they knew. If Briar had become a host while she was confined at the shelter, there was no telling who might be next. The Davis family had to be warned. Even if they didn't believe her story, she had to try.

KIM

KIM PLACED two wine glasses on the living room table alongside an open bottle of Nuits-Saint-Georges Tribourg 2012. She waited for her guest to arrive. When she heard the bell, she took her time down the stairs, pausing to count each one. She wanted to memorize all of the contours of her home.

"May I help you?" she asked the handsome silver-haired woman wearing a black trench coat.

"Hello. I'm sorry to trouble you. We've never met," the woman said. "My name is Mrs. Ted Van Devere. I'm acquainted with the Kenny family. We used to be neighbors. I live just up the road from you, at the Maplewood Mobile Home Park."

"I see," said Kim. "Well, come right in. I was about to indulge in a glass of wine. Won't you join me?" She led the way upstairs to the living room.

"You're too kind," said Mrs. Van Devere.

"No, please," said Kim. "My husband is on his way home. He must be stuck in traffic. It's awful, isn't it, this time of day? We often enjoy an after-work drink." She began pouring. "May I take your coat?"

"Thank you," said Mrs. Van Devere. She watched Kim place the coat carefully on the back of the sectional, and then she surveyed the place with one swift glance. "This is all very nice."

"The view is pretty, isn't it?" Kim asked. "We love this house, and the location. Have a seat." She held up her glass. "Now, let's see, this is a medium-bodied Burgundy with generous berry flavors and undertones of licorice, touched with a hint of oak. Tell me what you think."

Mrs. Van Devere took a drink. "Delicious," she said.

"Do you think so?"

"Yes," said Mrs. Van Devere. "Really, it's marvelous. Thank you." She took another sip while Kim settled in an armchair opposite her. "It might seem strange that I stopped by unannounced. I wouldn't blame you if you feel I'm an interfering old woman who should mind her own business."

Kim smiled and waited for Mrs. Van Devere to speak again. She detected a light fragrance emanating from the woman, and she wanted to say it was lavender. Her senses hadn't been so alive in years. She thought a teenage girl's awareness would be sharper than that of a woman in her thirties. She'd forgotten the madness of puberty, the kaleidoscope of moods and hormonal fluctuations. The open range ahead of her—the twenty-five years or so before meno-pause—suited her much better. She was feeling fit and unusually cheerful.

"Not at all," she assured Mrs. Van Devere. "We've been cut off here for a long time. You know what it's like raising children. You tend to forget the rest of the world."

"I suppose that's true," her guest agreed.

"Do you have children?"

"No," said Mrs. Van Devere. "I'm afraid not."

"What sort of work do you do?" Kim asked. "If you don't mind my nosiness."

"For a long time I was in cosmetic sales with a friend," said Mrs. Van Devere. "She relocated a few years ago, and I decided to retire. Are you in business, Mrs. Davis?"

Kim smiled at being addressed formally. "My contribution isn't worth mentioning, a little graphic design here and there. But I'm hoping to start painting again soon."

"Oh, are you an artist?"

Kim laughed. It struck her as absurd, the way the old woman pretended she was unfamiliar with the Davises and their history when she actually knew everyone in Skillute, alive and dead. Fortunately, she was growing less powerful as she aged, instead of sharpening her talents.

"I guess it's vain, isn't it?" asked Kim. "To tell people I'm an artist when I haven't made a name for myself."

"Maybe that's how one becomes an artist," said Mrs. Van Devere. "First you decide, then you declare yourself to the world, and then people pay attention."

"Well," said Kim, "let's just say, they haven't paid attention yet." She shifted in her seat. "What brings you here, aside from the chance to get acquainted, which I appreciate?"

"I apologize," said Mrs. Van Devere. "I should have stated my purpose right away. The reason for my visit is rather unpleasant."

"Oh?" Kim raised her eyebrows. She was getting the hang of it all faster than she expected.

"I understand Briar Kenny has been staying with your family."

Kim poured her guest a bit more wine, but said nothing.

"I visited with Briar while she was at Hope Haven," Mrs. Van Devere went on. "We had a long talk. I'm afraid she isn't exactly what she seems."

Kim looked at the old woman. She smiled. "Would you like a bite to eat?" she asked.

Mrs. Van Devere was puzzled for a moment. "No, thank you," she said. "This is a serious matter, Mrs. Davis."

"Call me Kim. Everyone calls me Kim, all of my friends."

"Kim," said Mrs. Van Devere. "I believe Briar Kenny is a dangerous person. She poses a grave threat to you and your family. No doubt this is shocking to hear, especially from a stranger. I weighed the consequences before deciding to speak to you."

Kim crossed her legs. "Consequences?"

"Yes," said Mrs. Van Devere. "You might not want the girl to live here, under your roof, once you recognize her true nature."

"What is her true nature?" Kim asked. She rested her elbow on her knee, and her chin on the palm of her hand.

"Evelyn Kenny has taken responsibility for the fire that killed her husband..."

"Boyfriend," said Kim.

"Yes," said Mrs. Van Devere. "Be that as it may, she told the police she had killed him when, in fact..."

"She murdered her husband Fred years ago," said Kim.

"I beg your pardon?" Mrs. Van Devere finished her wine and set the glass on the table. "This is a very..."

"Serious matter," said Kim. "Yes, you said so a minute ago. You believe people are running around Skillute, the most boring town on earth, murdering one another. You think the fourteen-year-old girl sharing a bedroom with my daughter and eating meals with my family is a cold-blooded killer. She murdered her stepfather. Is that it? Or is there more? Tell me there's more."

A sound from Tasha's bedroom stopped Kim in her tracks. She hesitated, unsure whether to investigate or to continue her conversation.

Mrs. Ted Van Devere reached inside her bag and retrieved a pair of bifocals. Her hands betrayed her with a slight tremble as she put them on.

"Is that better?" Kim asked. She leaned forward.

"Excuse me?"

"All the better to see me with, eh?" Kim asked with a grin.

"Who *are* you?" said the old woman.

"You can see me perfectly well," said Kim.

186

"Can I?" Mrs. Ted Van Devere asked.

"Yes!" Kim said. "Here I am—a healthy, attractive woman with money, talent, and a beautiful house. How long it's taken to get where I am right now!"

"Years, I expect," said her guest.

"Years and years and years! Oh, and I have a family. Do you think it's best to keep a family as a cover, or not? Most women want families, don't they? Most women expect other women to want a family. They're skeptical and cagey with a woman if she's content to be alone. You, for example, wandering the neighborhood, dressed in black, you'd attract less suspicion if you wore bright colors and told people you have six beautiful grandchildren. With that story, you could wheedle your way into anyone's home. As it is you're all too obviously a menace to decent folk, don't you think?"

"I've come too late, then," said Mrs. Ted Van Devere.

"Oh, yes!" said Kim. "Much too late. I'm surprised you bothered to stop by at all. Wasn't our conversation at the shelter enough to frighten you away? No? You still have faith in all of your mumbo-jumbo, you and your spell-casting girlfriends—or are they all dead? Isn't it time you joined them?"

Mrs. Van Devere held up her hands. She watched them trembling. Her head began to wobble.

"Your particular weakness is *luxury*, isn't it?" said Kim. "Inside your modest-looking trailer home you enjoy caviar and champagne. Your bathtub is a Jacuzzi and your bed is the finest money can buy. Of course you can't say no to a fine wine, even if instinct warns you not to indulge. Mrs. Dead Lavender, you shouldn't indulge yourself. You really are a nosy old witch. I'll bet you were dying to tell the police what you know, but who would believe it? So you pared your story down to a plausible warning about an awful teenager, a firebug, is that it? *Did you actually think I wouldn't hear you coming?*"

Mrs. Van Devere's mouth remained slightly open, but no sound came out. Her eyes were open, too, but they reflected nothing while Kim took hold of her by the shoulders and dragged her from the sectional, down the hall, toward her office at the back of the house.

"Not to worry, Dead Lavender," she said as she dragged the woman along. "You won't die from this. It's a lovely herbal mixture to knock you out so you won't feel a thing when I cut your throat. You can keep Briar company until the others arrive. She's comatose, so I'm afraid she isn't very talkative. Later we'll have a party, shall we? Or maybe I'll plant both of you in the yard. How about that? You can fertilize the tulips and maple trees and nightshade, like a good old girl."

First she'd have to deal with Charles. Then she could attend to the mess in her office. One thing at a time, she decided. Kim was a methodical artist. She would do one thing at a time.

CHARLES

CHARLES LET himself in and called out to Kim. "Where are you?"

Despite the hour, there was no sign of dinner in progress. He wondered if he was supposed to pick something up on the way. She hadn't said. It occurred to him that Tasha had grown sicker and had to go to the ER.

"Kim!" he called. "Kim!"

"I'm here. Upstairs!"

He bounded up the steps and found her in Tasha's room, sitting on one of the beds. She was drinking a glass of Chardonnay.

"Sorry," he said and kissed her on the cheek. "I got here as soon as I could."

"Oh, it's all right, now," said Kim. "I'm fine. I thought something happened to you, but here you are."

"The weirdest thing," he said. "There was a semi overturned on the freeway. Not just wrecked but flipped all the way over, upside down."

"How strange," said Kim, and sipped her wine.

"I had to slam on the brakes to avoid a couple of gawkers. People kept slowing down to see it."

"People are awful, aren't they?"

"The thing is, once I got close enough to see the cab of the truck, I could understand what all the fuss was about," he said. "The whole thing was covered in cottonwood."

"It's quite heavy this year, isn't it?" Kim said.

"No, you don't understand, this was just—crazy," he said. "It was all over the truck, so you could barely tell there was a vehicle underneath. It looked like a giant cocoon."

"That is odd, yes," said Kim. She tilted the glass and finished off the Chardonnay.

"Is Tasha in the bathroom?" Charles asked.

"No," said Kim.

"Where is she?" When Kim didn't answer, he asked again. "Where is Tasha?"

"I'm not sure, but I have a good idea," said Kim.

Charles shook his head. "Kim, what's going on? You called me and said to come home early, Tasha's not feeling well. Where is she?"

"Yes," she said. "That's right. I called you. I tucked her into bed. Then the doorbell rang."

"What?"

"The doorbell," said Kim. "Someone stopped by."

"What does that have to do with—? Who was it?"

"Oh," said Kim. "It doesn't matter, just a strange elderly woman selling cosmetics. Can you believe people still do that door-to-door? I told her we didn't need anything and she went away."

"Kim," Charles said. He took the wine glass from her hand and set it down on the dresser. "Where is Tasha? And where's Briar?"

"Oh, that little bitch," said Kim. "Briar. I told you she would be a nuisance, didn't I? She's nothing but trouble. We were fine before she came along."

Charles was taken aback. He put his hands on Kim's shoulders. He steadied himself.

"Where is our daughter?" he asked.

"Well," said Kim. "Let me think. Oh, yes. She went out."

"Out?"

"Yes," said Kim. "I sent the 'Avon lady' away. Then I poured myself a glass and sat down to wait for you. Later on, when I came in here to check on Tasha, she was gone."

"You didn't hear her leave?"

"No," said Kim. Her eyes opened and closed drowsily.

"Did you look for her? Did you check the whole house? Where's Briar?" Charles jumped up and started pacing. He ran a hand through his hair. "Kim, did you look for Tasha?"

"Of course, I searched everywhere," she said. "Inside, yes, and in the yard and the woods. Indoors, outdoors, all about the house! But I thought it was best to wait for you before running around the countryside."

He stopped pacing and stared at her. He hadn't seen her like this in many years, not since their baby had died and she'd completely closed down, leaving him stranded. He felt shut out now. The terrible part was, although he was the one left in the cold, it was up to him to solve the problem. This had been true throughout their life together. Kim was shattered, and Charles collected the pieces and put them together again.

He grasped the car keys in his pocket. "You say you know where she went?"

"Very likely," said Kim. "The place where she always goes with Briar. They probably went there together. It's that rundown cottage between the Cooper house and Curt Merritt's old barn. The yard's full of windmills and junk."

"How do you know about this?" Charles asked.

"Briar told me," said Kim. "She's a wealth of information once you crack her open."

Charles left Kim sitting on the bed. He didn't have time to worry about the state she was in. They could discuss all of it later, after he found Tasha.

CHARLES & TASHA

DESPITE HIS growing fear, Charles drove slowly. He was pretty sure where to find the house Kim had mentioned, but he knew how capricious kids could be. Tasha might have set out for one place and stumbled upon some distraction on the way.

This was an area he usually bypassed. Most of the houses were shuttered and falling down. He'd warned Tasha not to roam here.

Recently a new realty company had appeared, and was buying up lots as fast as they could locate the owners. Nobody knew what would take the place of the rundown homes of Skillute, but Charles expected the worst. Any day now he might look over from his deck—where he liked to enjoy his first cup of coffee in the morning—and see a Target sign where a stand of fir trees used to be.

It wasn't only the older part of town that was changing. Plenty of newer homes, built cheaply and occupied briefly by families in financial distress, had collapsed. After being stripped of all their plumbing and any fixtures worth a dime, they were usually gutted and knocked down. Skillute wasn't known for any natural resources except timber, and that was all but gone. What mattered to the realtors was the land itself, nothing residing on it and nothing underground.

The lots on all sides of the cottage were overgrown and vacant. Charles was able to recognize the place Kim described by the mass of clutter in front of it. The little picket fence bowed almost to the ground in several spots. The weeds owned the garden, winding through broken birdhouses and engulfing wooden geese, ducks, and bluebirds.

He might have guessed his daughter would choose to spend her time here. He could imagine her perched on a boulder or a bench, sketching, impervious to the melancholy nature of her surroundings. She would find all of it beautiful. His heart ached at the thought of her wandering here alone. How could Kim fail to notice when Tasha left the house? Was Briar with her? None of it made sense to Charles.

He parked the car, carefully avoiding a wide ditch. He didn't see the girls in the yard. He pushed the gate aside, letting it squeak gently onto the grass at a diagonal.

A pair of mourning doves murmured from a birdhouse on a tall post. When Charles stepped from the garden to the walkway, the doves nestled closer together. He had the uncomfortable sense that they were watching him, but he knew this was ridiculous. The whole town was like this, always had been. If ever he found himself alone, away from his home, he felt as if someone observed his movements, even his thoughts. Not with any specific intention, but with a voracious curiosity.

The idea was silly, and he'd never mentioned it to Kim or Tasha. They were more imaginative than he was, and the notion of a town having emotions and observations might trigger nightmares. They had all been through enough without adding paranoia to their dreams.

The door to the cottage was ajar. Inside was pitch black. Charles stepped closer and called out Tasha's name. His voice reverberated inside.

"Shit," he said. With a quick survey of the frame and general structure of the house, he pushed the door open wide and stepped across the threshold.

After a moment his eyes adjusted and shapes began to emerge from the gloom. Every inch of the rectangular room in which Charles stood was shrouded in dust and cobwebs. Still, he could recognize colors and objects beneath the grime: walls painted fuchsia and accentuated with gold leaf trim; broken Tiffany lamps in amber, lilac, and rose hues; moth-eaten tapestries and rugs. A few remnants of furniture—a large velvet sofa and armchairs—felt mossy to the touch. A sideboard and small table were covered in candles whose wax had long ago spilled over and left lumpy trails on the furniture's surface and the rugs below. There were mirrors on the walls, veined with gold leaf, all of them shattered. Above the fireplace the mantle was lined with cloudy glass bottles, silk tassels hanging from their necks, furry with spider webs. Atop one of these a black widow wiggled her legs, waiting for the next insect foolish enough to seek refuge.

The far wall was notable for an absence. There was a massive square patch where the fuchsia paint was more vibrant than anywhere else. Charles assumed a large painting had once occupied this central position in the room and had long since been removed. He heard scuffling and turned to see a raccoon digging at a hole in the corner. The animal gave him a fierce glance and disappeared into the hole.

"Tasha?" Charles called out. "Are you here? Tasha!"

"How did you find us?"

Charles turned and saw a pale girl with dirt on her chin, not his daughter, standing forlornly in the hall. From where he stood, the broken mirrors in the room caught her reflection and skewed it in a hundred directions. Behind her a shadow angled up the wall.

"Tasha!" he called out. "Where are you?" He turned to the girl, a skinny waif in a threadbare cotton dress. "Where is my daughter?" he asked the girl.

"I don't know," she said, and began to cry. Her shoulders shook.

Charles took a step toward the girl. The floorboards creaked and popped beneath his feet. When he was close enough to reach out and almost touch the girl, she looked up at him, and he realized she wasn't crying at all. She was grinning, and her teeth were stained with blood.

"Tasha!" he shouted. "Tasha!"

The girl giggled. She held out one hand full of dead flowers and twigs.

"Who are you?" Charles asked automatically, and took a step forward. Immediately he was grabbed by the ankles and tripped up. He fell on the floor with his palms open, landing hard. This prompted the girl to laugh.

When Charles raised his head and turned, he saw the silhouettes of what looked like two boys, one thick and heavy and the other taller and barrel-chested, squatting behind him. Both of them still held him by the ankles. The girl stood in front of Charles, wagging a finger at him.

"No, no," a voice whispered, but the girl's lips didn't move. "No heroes."

"Dad!" Tasha's voice screamed from somewhere in the house.

Charles scrambled to his knees and swiped at the silhouettes grasping his ankles. He was flailing, but his effort seemed to shake them loose. He climbed to his feet, took another step, and fell at once. As soon as he hit the floor, the two shadows were all over him, pinching and pushing and holding him down. He could hear the girl laughing. He rose up halfway and the shadows draped themselves over him. He opened his mouth to shout and felt their ice-cold fingers on his tongue. The more he moved the tighter they drew around him, closer to the skin, until he couldn't breathe.

He could hear Tasha crying and the sound forced him to move. He struck out at the shapes trying to hold and suffocate him. With all of his strength he rolled onto his back and punched and kicked— and suddenly they let go. They slithered away in all directions, and disappeared under the doors and into the corners.

"Dad!" Tasha screamed again.

He could see her trapped in the glittering light of the mirror, standing in the exact spot where the strange girl had stood, struggling to reach him. When she took a step toward him, he jumped to his feet and rushed to meet her, swept her up in his arms, and held her tight.

"It's okay," he told her. "I've got you. Everything's okay."

"Go away!" a woman's voice boomed from above and around them. "Get out of my house!"

Tasha was sobbing. Charles rushed outside with her and ran toward the car on the street. From the garden rose a cacophony of birdcalls, not songs but sounds of warning and distress, sounds of agony. The noise grew louder and shriller with every step Charles took.

He hoisted Tasha into the passenger seat and slammed the door shut. He only glanced at the garden as he rounded the car. It was silent now, and the door to the cottage was boarded up and nailed shut.

As soon as he climbed in he locked the doors, shoved the key into the ignition, and took off with tires squealing. Tasha wiped the tears from her face.

"What the hell were those things?" he asked. In the rearview mirror he saw three figures—children, standing in the garden, waving goodbye.

"I don't know," she said. "I don't know."

"What happened back there?"

"I don't know," Tasha told him. "How did you find me?"

"Your mother told me you would be here."

"How would she know?" Tasha asked. "Is Briar at home?"

"I haven't seen her," he admitted. "I thought she might have come here with you. Honey, what happened? Why did you run off like that? Why did you come to this place? What *is* this place?"

"I don't know."

Both of them were still shaking.

"I was so scared," Charles told her. "Kim said you were sick, and then she didn't know what happened to you."

"I woke up in my room," she said. "There was a woman talking to mom in the living room."

"She told me," said Charles. "Who was it?"

"A woman I didn't know. She said there was something wrong with Briar. I got scared. I don't know why I came here. I just ran. I went to the cottage and the door was open. It's never open. I peeked inside and something grabbed me. It wouldn't let me go! Dad, it was never going to let me go!"

"Okay," said Charles. "Okay. It's all right now, honey. It's okay. You're here with me. You're safe. We're going home."

He steered past the ruins of Jessup's Diner. He drove by the freeway exit and turned down the street toward their house.

It occurred to Charles that the immediate priority was to get Tasha home and help her to calm down. This was more important than figuring out whatever the hell was going on inside that cottage. Later he'd call the police and have them ransack the place. If they couldn't find out what was going on, he would, or he'd burn the place to the ground. In fact, the more he thought about what had just happened, the more he wanted to burn the place down. But first he had to take care of his daughter. "Let's go home and we can talk about it. Are you feeling okay?"

"Yeah," she said. "My head feels funny, but I'm okay."

As they approached their house, Charles noticed another car parked on the street. He didn't recognize it. "You told me a woman came to the house. What exactly did the woman say to Kim about Briar?" he asked. "Can you remember?"

Tasha nodded but didn't say anything.

"It's all right if you don't remember," Charles told her. "You're not feeling well. It's okay."

"No," said Tasha. "I remember. She said Briar killed her stepdad. She set the fire on purpose, not her mother. She was lying, wasn't she? That was a lie, right?"

"Yeah," he said, because all he wanted was to protect Tasha from any more pain. "Yeah, the woman must have been confused. She didn't know what she was saying."

"It was a lie," Tasha said to herself. "It was a lie."

THE DAVIS
FAMILY

"HELLO!" KIM'S voice greeted them brightly when they walked through the door into the foyer. She was waiting, and she threw her arms around Tasha.

"Baby! I was so worried!" she said.

"Mom!" Tasha cried out. "It was horrible!"

"Oh my god," said Kim. She gave Charles a look of concern. "Are you all right?"

"We're okay," said Charles. "I'll tell you all about it later. Let's get Tasha to bed."

Tasha leaned against her mother. She let Kim squeeze her tight and inhale the scent of her hair and skin.

Charles put a hand on Kim's shoulder. "How are you feeling?" he asked.

"Better now," she said, her arms still wrapped around Tasha. "I'm sorry I was out of it before. Everything happened at once. I was upset, and ashamed. I didn't know what to do, how to handle things."

"It's okay," he said. He'd made allowances for far worse. He could weather a mood. It was nothing compared to all they'd been through together. It was nothing compared to what he'd just seen in a darkened house less than three miles from his own home.

"Let's get you upstairs," Kim said to Tasha.

"I don't want to be alone," Tasha said.

"You don't have to be," said Kim. "We can camp out in the living room. I'll get you some bottled water and a bowl of soup. We can rent a movie, anything you like."

Kim had one foot on the stairs, a bright smile shining from her face. Charles kissed the back of her neck. He would wait for Tasha to be settled in before he called the police. If anything else threatened to disrupt their lives, he would deal with it alone.

They ascended the stairs together, touching as though afraid letting go would cause some new and unknown disaster. In the living room Charles and Tasha collapsed onto the sectional. Kim fetched Tasha a cup of herbal tea, and poured a glass of wine for Charles. He drank it quickly and poured another while Tasha sipped her tea.

"That's better," said Kim. "Just rest and relax. Everything can wait until tomorrow. We can sort all of it out in the morning."

Charles knew he had much more to do, but he wanted more than anything to rest. Beyond the window, the cottonwood was starting to swirl like the first downy flakes of a blizzard about to break.

"Where's Briar?" Tasha asked.

Kim's smile remained, but now it was hard and brittle, as if it had become stuck. Charles and Tasha waited. From some part of the house there was a sort of clicking and grinding, like the inner workings of a large clock.

"She's gone," said Kim. "She left after you went to bed this afternoon. I'm sorry. I'm so sorry. I didn't want you to worry. I guess I was hoping she would change her mind and come back before you got home."

"Change her mind about what? What do you mean?" Tasha said. "She's gone? Where?"

Kim stopped smiling and said, "I don't know. She was angry. We had a talk after that woman left. I don't know. The woman was odd, and she made some accusations. I had a talk with Briar. She blew up at me. She said she hated living here and she called someone to pick her up."

Tasha was dumbfounded. "Who picked her up? She doesn't have any family."

"Well," said Kim, "apparently that was a lie. A nice lady in a station wagon with a couple of kids and a dog in it came to collect her and said she'd call the social worker to let her know where Briar would be living."

"How could you let her do that?" Charles asked.

"Where did they go?" Tasha asked. "Did she leave a phone number?"

"No," said Kim. "That's why I was in such a state when you got home, Charles. The whole thing seemed crazy, and Tasha was gone, and I was scared to death. But these people in the car knew Briar and Briar knew them. She wanted to leave. You weren't here. I couldn't stop her."

"We should contact the authorities," Charles said. "It doesn't sound right." His thoughts were growing fuzzy.

"What doesn't sound right?" Kim asked. "What about it doesn't sound right?"

"The whole story," he said. "It doesn't make sense. What happened at that cottage doesn't make sense. All of it, it's crazy!"

Kim gave him a cool look. Tasha turned slowly from one to the other of her parents, waiting for answers.

"Yes," said Kim. "Yes. My god! You're right. Let's call the police and find out what's going on, tomorrow morning, bright and early. Now, come on. You know what people say. Chicken soup is good for the soul. Family is where we all belong. A good night's sleep will put all of us in a better mood. There's nothing like it."

She went to the kitchen, leaving Charles and Tasha to stare after her.

"Dad," said Tasha.

"Yeah, honey?" His words were becoming harder to form. He had no idea what to do next.

"Dad," Tasha said again. "What's wrong with Mom?"

"What do you mean?" he asked, trying not to make things worse. If he could sit quietly for a while, maybe he could sort it all out.

Tasha glanced in the direction of the kitchen. Then she leaned close to him. She whispered, "Something's wrong. Don't you feel it?"

"Mom's been having a rough time lately," said Charles, but his reassurance was hollow. He knew she was right. From the kitchen he could hear Kim humming and moving things around.

"I know, but..." Tasha glanced toward the kitchen again. "This is different. Can't you feel it?"

"Let's indulge her, okay?" Charles said wearily. "I'm sorry about your friend, but it sounds like she's going to be all right. I'm sure she'll call in a few days, when she gets settled."

"I don't know. I hope so," said Tasha. "There was something she wanted me to know."

"What? Did she say what it was about?"

"No, but I gave her a keepsake. My bracelet, remember?" Tasha paused as if something important, something that had slipped her mind, hovered at the edge of her consciousness. "We were talking in my room when I got sick. Something weird happened..."

He didn't ask any more. He was well aware of the meaning behind the bracelet. Like Kim, he had assumed it was long forgotten, lost along with dozens of toys and mementoes over the years. He didn't want to prompt her to think about it.

"Never mind," said Charles. "We've been through enough, haven't we?"

She nodded, but her face was pale.

He put an arm around her shoulders. He took a deep breath. As always, from the day she became his child until this moment, he knew he couldn't keep her from the truth. It would come eventually, no matter what he did to try and prevent it. All he could do was postpone the inevitable and hope for the best, hope she would forgive him.

"Remember when you were little and I used to read you a story every night?" he asked.

She nodded. The humming in the kitchen grew louder and the clicking and grinding of gears in another room began again.

"We would pile all your stuffed toys around you in bed, so nothing bad could happen, and everyone would sleep safe and sound?" He watched the swirls of cottonwood outside. They were growing thicker.

"Dad," said Tasha. She looked drowsy, unable to hold her head steady. "Where do you think Briar went?"

"Someplace safe," he lied. "Someplace good. Where good children sleep soundly in their own beds..." He realized the humming was louder now, and Kim was somewhere at the back of the house, fumbling with things in her office. It occurred to him that this might be the last time he was able to act, to stop whatever was coming, but he didn't have the strength to stand. He couldn't even raise his arms.

"Kim?" he tried to call out, but his voice was a whisper. It fell away like dust.

He turned to Tasha and saw she was asleep. Her head was tilted back, resting against the cushions, and her mouth was opened slightly.

"Kim?" he said.

The fumbling noises continued. This time he couldn't tell where they were coming from. It seemed as if the whole house were whispering and groaning on its foundation, threatening to slide away.

Outside, cottonwood filled the sky beyond the deck. The air was blank white with the fibers, with no separation between them. Charles could feel his body slipping into deep sleep, and there was nothing he could do about it. Whatever was to come, whatever was creeping inexorably toward him from every corner of the house, he was powerless to stop it.

ACKNOWLEDGEMENTS

Thank you to my husband, Cory J. Herndon, for the life we share. Thank you to my wonderful editor, Jess Landry, for good questions, good advice, and infinite patience. And thanks to Scarlett R. Algee for the meticulous proofreading. Cheers to Trepidatio for loving and sharing the horror.

S.P. Miskowski is a recipient of two National Endowment for the Arts Fellowships. Her stories have been published in *Supernatural Tales, Black Static, Identity Theory, Strange Aeons* and *Eyedolon Magazine,* and in numerous anthologies including *The Best Horror of the Year Volume Ten, Haunted Nights, The Madness of Dr. Caligari, October Dreams 2, Autumn Cthulhu, The Hyde Hotel, Darker Companions: Celebrating 50 Years of Ramsey Campbell, Tales from a Talking Board* and *Looming Low.*

Her second novel, *I Wish I Was Like You,* won This Is Horror 2017 Novel of the Year and a Charles Dexter Award for Favorite Novel of 2017 from *Strange Aeons Magazine.* Her books have received three Shirley Jackson Award nominations and a Bram Stoker Award nomination, and are available from Omnium Gatherum Media and JournalStone/Trepidatio.

CPSIA information can be obtained
at www.ICGtesting.com
Printed in the USA
FFHW020806040519
52240691-57634FF